DEADWATER

DEADWATER

ANTHONY GIANGREGORIO

Copyright © 2006 by Anthony Giangregorio.

ISBN 10:   Softcover   1-4257-3645-9

ISBN 13:   Softcover   978-1-4257-3645-3

All rights reserved. No part of this book may be reproduced or transmitted in any form or by any means, electronic or mechanical, including photocopying, recording, or by any information storage and retrieval system, without permission in writing from the copyright owner.

This is a work of fiction. Names, characters, places, and incidents either are the product of the author's imagination or are used fictitiously, and any resemblance to any actual persons, living or dead, events, or locales is entirely coincidental

This book was printed in the United States of America.

To order additional copies of this book, contact:
Xlibris Corporation
1-888-795-4274
www.Xlibris.com
Orders@Xlibris.com

ACKNOWLEDGEMENTS

SPECIAL THANKS TO: Mike Shea for all the support he's given me; Joe Grondin for helping with the technical stuff; my mom for reading an early draft and giving me her "real" opinion; my wife Jody for her support throughout this whole project; to all my friends who read rough drafts of parts of this book and gave me your unbiased input; and especially to Michelle Jesse for her hand painted artwork displayed on the cover, you can contact her at Medea_q3@hotmail.com.

FOREWORD

FOR THE LOVE OF ZOMBIES

I LOVE ZOMBIE movies, ever since in 1984 when I first sat down and watched George Romero's Dawn of the Dead for the first time I was hooked.

Recently I have been researching more literature on zombies and it really made me think about how they fit into our present culture.

Why do I always have to mumble under my breath when someone asks me what my favorite movies are?

Why is it that out of all the people I know I can only count two or three other people who are as passionate about zombies as I am?

Why is it that the common mechanic will watch his Texas chainsaws and new cuts of Hills but when I say there's a new zombie movie out they look at me like I'm nuts?

Ever since I was about seventeen I was fascinated with death. I remember going down to the local video store and searching endlessly for new copies of the Faces of Death. Its not that I got off on watching dead people—real dead people—on the screen, it's more like I enjoyed being reminded of my own mortality.

After I would watch one of those videos I would walk around with a feeling of "it's so good to be alive" when it seems fate could snatch it away at any second.

Which brings me back to zombies movies and why I love them so.

A zombie movie is make believe. The dead probably aren't going to be getting up anytime soon and start walking around. And that people is why the gorier the better because it's not real and it never will be.

Now slasher flicks and your Texas Chainsaw's why a little extreme do happen. Take Ted Bundy for instance. What that man did to innocent people puts your worst zombie to shame easily.

What happens in these slasher movies do happen and God help us all will happen again, can anyone say Manson family?

So then why does everyone embrace these movies so much and leave the zombie by the side of the road?

The thing about zombies is that they are so far removed from reality that you can get lost in this fantasy world where the dead walk and your nine to five jobs don't exist anymore.

Where the everyday drudge to work becomes a fight for survival, and though of course I don't want to see the end of the world happen, wouldn't it be nice to just break off the chains of society that weigh each and every one of us down? And who among us has never had a jerk of a neighbor or a really mean person in your school where in all reality the only way to get rid of them is to be violent.

But you can't! In this "civilized world" we have all been thrown into the way of "only the strong survive" has been replaced by, "I'll see you in court."

But I digress, although it still cuts to the heart of this subject. If a zombie gets in your way, shoot it in the head. If you don't have a gun well that's ok, got a machete handy? Well get busy buddy and start choppin' until that head's clean off. So where you or I would never do something like that in the real world (hopefully) in the world of zombies it's as natural as waking up every morning.

That simple animal inside us all, well probably mostly men anyway, can sit back and revel in a zombie movie as the fight to survive takes on its most basic level.

Remember this people. Every day in the news you hear about another tragic murder of someone. And when the news focuses on the story more we all end up seeing the darker side of humanity each and every day.

My point being, when was the last time the news covered the latest zombie outbreak?

I recently found out that there are zombie books that you can read. Whole story's of the living dead just waiting at the local bookstore for you to pick up and enjoy anytime you want, and so far they've been better than most of the movies out there.

In fact I was so inspired after reading these books that I too sat down and transcribed a story of the undead.

This brings me back to the whole reason for this story. When I would share with friends and acquaintances that I had started writing a book there eyebrows would always go up for a moment and ask me what I was writing about. The moment I said a story about zombies there eyebrows would drop back down and they would immediately lose interest.

Why I ask? I know there are fellow minded people like me out there. I'm telling you if we all banded together we would be a force to be reckoned with.

One person even told me "Zombies? Wow, I wouldn't spread that around."

So if you're a zombie fan great, there needs to be more of us out there and if your not, well, my friends you don't know what your missing.

In closing I'd like to add one more thing, a friend and I were talking about zombie movies and books and why I was so passionate about them and he asked me:

"But why do you like them so much, what do you get out of them?"

And I replied. "If you have to ask, then it just doesn't really matter."

Anthony
Giangregorio
September 2006

CHAPTER 1

HENRY WATSON ROLLED over in bed, while burying his head deeper under the pillows. The sun's light was blasting into his bedroom through the room's front window. He new he should get up, but didn't want to.

Downstairs he could hear his wife Emily tinkering around in the kitchen making breakfast.

The smell of coffee floated up the stairs, enticing him to get up. "No not yet," he thought, just a few more minutes. Then he felt the pressure on his bladder worsen as he shifted position in bed again. Great, now he had to go to the bathroom.

After waiting another minute or so he gave in.

"Time to get up and face the day," Emily would say every morning when she herself got up.

"Huh, face the day, what a load of bull." He thought.

As he went into the bathroom his mind went back two weeks ago, he had been just about to leave work and go home for the weekend. It had been a long week.

He had put in at least an extra fifteen hours over his expected fifty and because he was salary he wasn't going to get one extra dollar in his paycheck, but hey, that's life in the real world. You don't always get what you deserve.

He had been a software programmer for going on twelve years now and although it wasn't glamorous it paid the bills (quite well actually) and he was good at it. So to say that it surprised the hell out of him to find out his company was closing down and moving to India of all places, totally blew him away. At least he had received a generous severance package and when that ran out there was always unemployment insurance.

After finishing in the bathroom he headed downstairs to see his wife, as he rounded the corner from the stairs he could see she had just finished preparing breakfast.

It smelled good, she had made bacon and eggs and toast. Unfortunately the bacon was that low cholesterol crap that looked like bacon but tasted liked she took one of his old shoes and fried it up. He would always eat it though, after all she meant well and he loved her.

For the hundredth time since he had found out his cholesterol was high he wondered why everything that was supposed to be good for you tasted like shit.

"Well, well, look who decided to get up; you looked so sweet I didn't have the heart to wake you." She said as she put two plates on the table.

"You feel any better this morning?" Emily asked in that perky tone of hers.

"Yeah I'm fine, don't worry I'll be okay, I figure I might as well enjoy being home while I can." He said as he sat down at the kitchen table.

"The mortgage bill came in today.' She said quietly.

Henry frowned and said: "Now don't worry Emily, we're doing fine, I have plenty of money in the checking account to pay it."

But Emily wouldn't let up. "Ok, this month is covered, but what about next month?"

Henry's face darkened as he looked at his wife. "We'll be fine next month too, now will you please lay off with the money worries?"

Emily looked down for a moment and then tactfully changed the subject "So," Emily smiled, "have you thought about coming with me to see my mother next week?"

"Great," Henry thought Emily's mom gave him shit when he had a job; he couldn't wait to hear what she'd say when she found out he was now unemployed. So instead of answering her he picked up the remote for the kitchen television and turned on the news.

There was a terror alert on, not that that's such a big deal anymore, lately the media had been issuing alerts for every reason under the sun, and besides what the hell could he do about it anyway? He changed the channel to see what else was on while Emily chatted away.

Emily kept going on about her night out with the girls last night. He made sure he nodded and uhuh-ed when appropriate and mainly concentrated on changing the television channels.

When he finished breakfast he got up and went to give his wife her regular kiss on the cheek.

"I'm gonna go run a few errands Hun'. I'll be back in a couple of hours," Henry said.

"Okay I'll see you later," she said over her shoulder as she went to work clearing the breakfast table. "Would you pick up a gallon of milk on your way home today?"

"Sure, no problem Hun'," he answered back while scooping his keys off the wall.

Before he walked out the back door he turned to her and said: "Hey, you know we're gonna be fine, don't you?"

She smiled back and answered: "Yes I suppose I do, I just can't help worrying a little. She blew him a kiss. "Now you go on and run your errands and I'll see you later."

As Henry walked out to his car he had no idea that he would never see his wife alive again.

CHAPTER 2

PINERIDGE LABORATORIES WAS a sprawling five acre ranch that specialized in chemical and biological contagions like so many other laboratories across these United States, the American public had no idea of what the real function these labs performed, and Pineridge labs was no exception.

Jimmy cooper had been an unhappy employee for the last six months, the only reason he even started working here is because he was tired of his dad busting his balls to get a job, so when dear old dad cut of his allowance he didn't really have a choice.

His dad got him a job here thanks to an old army buddy who worked security here. Unfortunately there were no jobs open in security so poor Jimmy had to settle for janitorial duties.

It wasn't too bad usually; Jimmy got to screw off a lot after Mr. Dawson (the head janitor) went home for the day.

Although being at the bottom of the food chain can suck too; such as the way the Docs treated him, like he was no better than a stain on the wall.

Usually he just let it slide but after six months of taking their shit he was really ready to quit this job and move on. To what who the hell knows, but the grass is always greener on the other side. So when he got to work this morning and Mr. Dawson told him to go clean Ward six he nearly shit his pants, no one gets into Ward six unless you've been employed at Pineridge for at least one year with no mistakes on your record and a receive a full security check.

Or so Jimmy found out at Mr. Dawson's office.

"We need you to fill in for Tommy, Jimmy," said Mr. Dawson. "He broke his leg and we're short staffed so I'm promoting you to Ward six."

"Thanks Mr. Dawson, that's great I could use the raise," said Jimmy.

"So head over there now and see Dr. Martin, he'll tell you what your duties are." said Mr. Dawson. Jimmy left the office and headed for Ward six thinking that maybe he'd stick around after all. If he did a good job maybe he could stay in Ward six even after Tommy came back.

Dr. Martin was a tiny man with a pale complexion and thick coke bottle glasses, the kind of kid in school Jimmy would have beat up for his lunch money, but now this geek was Jimmy's boss.

"Hello Jimmy, I'm Dr. Martin," he said holding out his hand for Jimmy to shake. Jimmy shook his hand. It was like shaking wet, loose spaghetti. As Jimmy inconspicuously wiped his hand on the back of his pants he said hi back and asked what his duties would be.

"Well Jimmy we do a lot of work with bacteria in this section of the labs such as ways to clean up polluted water and sewage using natures own tools, with a little help from man of course." He chuckled to himself.

Jimmy just smiled back, not really getting the joke and thinking what a dork this guy is.

"Your duties will be the usual janitorial duties plus assisting me and my staff by running errands such as coffee, lunches ect . . ."

"Sure Dr. M no problem, whatever you need me to do, just name it," said Jimmy.

Dr. Martin frowned by the slang use of his name by Jimmy but let it go.

The phone on his desk began to ring and Dr. Martin answered it and Jimmy was immediately forgotten.

After a few minutes Jimmy was pretty sure Dr. Martin was done with him so he slowly raised himself out of his chair and with a wave left the office.

Dr. Martin barely noticed him leave as he was so absorbed in his phone call.

Jimmy strolled down the hallway, trying to think of a place he could screw off for a while. "I know," he said to himself. "The basement."

As he felt in his back pocket to make sure his joint was still there he headed off for the hatch to the basement, whistling as he walked.

And so started Jimmy's promotion at Pineridge and the beginning of the end of the world.

CHAPTER 3

MARY ROBERTS LOOKED up from her desk in the lobby at Pineridge laboratories to look at the clock. The minute hand was just shy of ten o clock.

She sighed to herself, counting how many more hours left until five o clock.

Although being the receptionist at Pineridge wasn't a demanding job, as there was no walk in traffic due to Pineridge being a private research facility, it did sometimes get boring.

Her main responsibilities consisted of answering the phone and receiving packages. Nothing out of the ordinary for a receptionist although some of the visitors looked a little too mysterious for her liking.

They always had that stereotypical G-man look with the black suit and the dark sunglasses and the always serious demeanor, but they were always polite if not very talkative, such as the fellow who had just entered the lobby, he was dressed in a crisp black suit and dark glasses; of course, with a short military style haircut. He walked up to her and stopped at her desk.

"Good morning, I'm her to see Dr. Martin, he's expecting me," he smiled.

Mary smiled back. "Just one minute sir let me call Dr. Martin and see where he is."

After confirming that the Dr. was on his way down she signed him in and gave him his security badge, by the time she had finished the elevator door chimed open and out came Dr. Martin wearing a smile from ear to ear.

"Ah, Mr. Jacobs, how nice to see you again please come with me and I'll fill you in on the progress we've made."

He waved bye to Mary as he escorted Jacobs to the elevator. The minute the doors closed Jacobs turned and looked straight at Dr. Martin.

"You better have something to show me or else I can pretty much guarantee your funding will be pulled Dr. Martin. My employers and your benefactors are expecting results not more bullshit about how close you are to a breakthrough."

The elevator had come to a stop and Martin exited the elevator with Jacobs behind him. At the end of the hall stood a set of metal double doors with a card swipe on the right.

Martin swiped it and when the light turned green the doors swung open. Both men nearly walked into Jimmy who had his head buried in a comic book. At the last second Jimmy looked up and stopped, "Hey Mr. D, I was gonna take my break now." Jimmy said.

"Yes, yes fine just don't go far. I need you to straighten up one of the labs in a little while."

"Sure Mr. D. no problem I'll be back in fifteen or so." Jimmy said as he headed down the corridor towards the elevator, where he thought he'd kill his break talking to Mary.

Mary looked up as the elevator doors opened and saw Jimmy walking towards her.

"Hi Mary, how's it going?" Jimmy asked her as he walked over to her desk.

"Hi Jimmy," Mary smiled, "Fine I guess, you?"

"Same shit different day, hey how about that suit I saw Dr. Martin with, he sure looked intense, like one of those guys in those G-man movies."

"Mary smiled, "I see those guys all the time, they must have Dr. Martin doing something important. They've been coming by a lot more often lately."

"Yeah well I guess that's why Dr. M. and the other scientists get paid the big bucks, I'm gonna get something to drink, you want anything?"

"Yes please, could you get me a bottle of water?"

"Water, why would you buy water when it's free from any water fountain in here?"

"I don't drink water from the tap it has all kinds of chemicals in it, that's why I only drink bottled water, it's better for you."

"Whatever, I'll see what I can do."

"Why don't you grab one for yourself Jimmy, it's my treat." She said as she handed him a five dollar bill.

"Sure why not. Jimmy said as he walked off to the break room to retrieve the beverages.

As Jimmy went to get the drinks he didn't realize he had just received the best advice of his young life.

CHAPTER 4

HENRY TURNED RIGHT onto Main St. and headed into town. He figured he'd park on Main St. and walk around for awhile. Maybe go to the park and watch the kids play. He and his wife never had kids, not because they didn't want too, but it just never seemed the right time; then before you know it your forty-five and childless.

Not that it's so bad, his brother Billy had two kids and he spent time with them so he did get to spend time with children, although not as much as he'd like. His job always kept him pretty occupied, although that hadn't been a problem until recently.

"Bastards," he muttered, "Twelve friggin' years down the drain."

He headed down into the park where the kids were playing in the water fountains. People were everywhere today, walking dogs, jogging, and his favorite, the fast walkers.

He stopped by a vendor selling refreshments and bought a bottle of water; ever since he was a kid he'd hated tap water. The small town he'd lived in had added fluoride to the town's water supply so when he had moved out he'd promised himself he would never drink tap water again.

His wife thought he was silly but being that he didn't have too many quirks she indulged him.

Even to the point of getting water delivered every week to the house.

As he walked deeper into the park he spotted a father and son playing catch together. The boy was around five years old and every time he would drop the ball his father would run over to him and show him how to catch it. Then he'd ruffle his hair and jog back to where he'd been standing and they'd try again.

Henry watched them for a while and then continued on into the park.

He spotted two young lovers curled up in a blanket under a big oak tree.

He couldn't see much of the couple as they were under the blanket but he had a pretty good idea of what they were doing.

He smiled to himself, thinking of Emily and himself when they were young.

Those were good times.

All around him was the sound of laughter and joy. Henry took a swig from the bottle and walked deeper into the park. Even though he had started today in a bad mood it was just so pleasant in the park it was hard to stay miserable and as he continued into the park he felt his mood lightening.

Maybe today wouldn't be so bad after all.

CHAPTER 5

WHEN JIMMY RETURNED from his break he caught up with Dr. Martin, who told him to go to room two and mop the floors and empty the trash buckets. The usual stuff, what was weird was the warning Jimmy got from him.

"Jimmy," Martin said with concern on his face." Be careful not to disturb anything on the tables, the contents are very important to my research. I probably shouldn't even have you in there unsupervised but I just don't have the time to do those things myself. Mr. Dawson cleared you to work in this Ward so I don't believe there should be any problem, if anything should arise contact me immediately."

"And remember, Jimmy, don't touch anything."

"Jimmy had replied: "Not to worry Dr. M. it's all under control."

Martin just grunted a "See that it is," and then headed away down the hallway, muttering to himself about deadlines and funding.

After a quick detour to grab the janitorial cart and his headphones Jimmy headed over to room two.

When he entered the room his nose was immediately assaulted by the smell in the room, it smelled like dead animals left in the sun. There were aquarium tanks all over the room with things floating in them, and tubes coming of the tops going into other containers. Over in the corner was a fifty gallon tank. He couldn't really see what it contained as the water was murky; whatever was in it looked big enough to be a body. He chuckled to himself, dismissing the thought immediately. "That's ridiculous," he said under his breathe and went back to work cleaning up.

He put his headphones on and started mopping the floor, the task was actually a little more complicated than it should have been due to all the tubes coming out of the tanks, some of which were hanging by the floor. He was jamming' to his favorite rock band and a real cool guitar solo came up so like most guys Jimmy's age he whipped the mop up and started to rip some air guitar. What he didn't notice was that he had wandered a little too close to the big tank in the corner and when he whipped the mop up the handle caught one of the tubes hanging off the tank. As the tube broke a brown liquid began pouring out. At first it settled in the corner but soon the dark mass overflowed and started seeping down the floor drain. Nearly half of the tank was empty when Jimmy turned around and saw his mistake.

"Oh shit," he gasped "I am so fuckin dead."

A million thoughts went through his mind in a flash about what was going to happen to him when Dr. Martin came back.

He ran over to the tank and placed the hose back into its connector. As he got closer the odor of decay was even worse; he was able to see what was in the tank better now as most of the liquid was gone. To his astonishment it was a dead body. Or what was left of one.

The skin on the skull looked more like leather than skin. The eye sockets were sunken in with the soft tissue like eyeballs having rotted away into the muck. The head of the corpse was at a slight angle and to Jimmy looked almost like a grotesque mimicry of sleep. The rest of the body was still submerged in the sludge so he couldn't tell if it was male or female, and frankly he didn't care.

He looked around the room thinking about how he was going to cover his ass and fix this problem when he saw the water hose next to the sink. An idea came to him immediately; he headed over and grabbed the hose, connected it to the faucet and ran the other end into the tank.

As the hose started filling the tank he retrieved a sguigy from his cart and started scraping the sludge off the floor and into the drain, the smell was awful so he grabbed some ammonia and poured it on the floor and down the drain to cut down on the smell. There were some other unmarked bottles on the shelf and he grabbed these as well and poured them down the drain not caring what they were in his panic to hide his mistake.

By the time the tank was filled back to the line that had been left on the tank when it had drained Jimmy had hurled three times due to the smell, the ammonia barely helped to cut the odor and putting his nose and mouth inside his shirt did nothing to help.

He grabbed the hose and washed the floor down one more time, he was out of ammonia so he threw down the rest of the contents of the unmarked bottles and then mopped and sguigyed all the residue down the drain. He had just finished the last swipe of the mop when Dr. Martin walked in.

"Are you finished Jimmy, I need to get back to work in here and I don't need you distracting me?" Dr. Martin said impatiently, as his nose wrinkled at the smell of the ammonia in the air.

"Sure am Dr. Martin let me just empty these trash barrels and I'll be out of your hair." Jimmy said until he looked at Dr. Martin's incredibly receding hairline.

"Oh sorry man, you know what I mean."

"Dr. Martin just frowned at him.

Jimmy finished emptying the barrels in silence, figuring he'd said enough.

When he finished he grabbed his cart and as he was wheeling it out took one last look over his shoulder at Dr. Martin.

Dr. Martin was in the corner by the big tank writing something on a clipboard and thank god he wasn't noticing anything unusual.

Jimmy smiled to himself, "Holy shit, I can't believe I got away with that," he thought, as he headed down the corridor.

At the moment he was on top of the world.

Unfortunately that feeling wasn't gong to last.

CHAPTER 6

THE BUILDING PINERIDGE labs occupied had been standing since the early 1950's. Originally it had been used as a turkey farm until the early 1960's when the family sold the building and moved to Florida to enjoy their golden years in the sun. The building sat empty for a few years until in the late 60's a pharmaceutical company purchased it. When the pharmaceutical company moved on in the middle of 1970 Pineridge labs took over and has been the buildings occupants ever since.

Through all of this the buildings sewer system remained untouched, where zoning laws today would never allow open drain pipes to filter into to the town's water supply the building had actually had two that did. They were relatively small and were basically dormant.

The exit spouts were hidden from view due to all the overgrown foliage so had remained undetected all these years.

This morning one of those pipes was in use. All the tank water and ammonia and unnamed chemicals that Jimmy had disposed of gushed out of the spout and poured into the town's reservoir. Upon hitting the water the effluent matter immediately started multiplying. The bacteria and enzymes that were in the toxic soup from Dr. Martins experiment began mutating thanks to the extra cleaning supplies Jimmy had added. Where ammonia would normally have a nullifying effect on bacteria, this new strain thrived on it. Immediately a translucent like algae began forming on the surface of the lake, growing larger and larger as the minutes past.

Seconds later the marine life started floating to the surface; they twitched for a moment and then remained still. A flock of birds that had stopped by for a quick dip and had then flown back into the air started twitching in flight and then as one fell back to the earth to land in the lake with barely a splash to mark their landing.

A deer had come to the water's edge to drink the cool water, after moments of its first drink it suddenly shook and then fell to the ground and remained still.

Its chest rose and fell from it's breathing for only seconds before becoming inanimate.

Within the hour the entire lake was tinted a light shade of green and the pumping facility started sending the contaminated water out to the towns' water pipes. The pipes sending it to every sink, water fountain and hose spicket in the town and the surrounding areas.

The surrounding woods were still; no birds chirped and no squirrels foraged.

As if the wildlife could feel the impending doom approaching.

CHAPTER 7

HENRY WOKE UP with a start. A dog had jumped to close to him while trying to catch a stick and had startled him. He brushed sleep from his eyes and looked up at the sun. It had definitely moved a ways across the sky. He checked his watch and sure enough he had been asleep for a little over an hour and a half.

After walking around the park for an hour or so he had gotten tired so had sat down on a park bench for a rest and sure enough he had dozed off. His wife would always tease him about how he could fall asleep anywhere. The movie theatre was the worst; put him in a dark room with a comfortable chair, and he'd be out in ten minutes, no matter what was playing on the screen.

He got up and decided to start for home. On his route back he passed by a big water fountain where all the kids would come and play on a warm day; there were still about seven or eight kids playing in the water although as he looked at the moms they seemed to be the exhausted ones. He smiled to himself as he thought if he could invent a device to harness the energy of all children he'd be rich.

All of a sudden all the kids in the fountain stopped playing and just stood there, the silence hanging in the air, and then all at once the kids fell to the ground like a light a switch had been turned off.

The kids moms and dads all jumped up and ran to their prospective children while yelling "oh my gods" and calling their children's names. Henry noticed one mom who was quicker than the others run up and pick up her son in her arms. He was a cute little boy of about eight. As Henry got closer he could see that his eyes were closed like he was sleeping, as were the other kids.

Try as they could, between yelling and shaking the kids nothing was working. Henry watched as the mother of the eight year old boy hugged him to her, telling him it would be alright and for the first few seconds panicking. She was rummaging in her jacket-probably for a cell phone—Henry thought—when he saw the boy's eyes snap open. For a second he just stared at his mother and then with no warning his mouth opened and his jaw went straight for her neck. Henry just stared in shock as the boys head pulled back taking a one inch size hole out of the side of her neck. As she started screaming the boy went back in for more, ripping another inch from her throat. Her screams didn't last long as her son had ripped into her jugular and the blood was coming out so fast she was literally dead on her feet. The boy was immediately covered in his mother's blood.

For one split second the parents didn't move. Then as if by another switch one after the other all of the kids eyes opened and after a pause, almost like a reset button being pushed, one by one the children attacked anyone that was close to them.

Two children who were probably brother and sister knocked over their father and before he had a chance to push them off each child had ripped an eyeball out, to the background of the screams of their father they devoured his eyes like they were a couple of gumballs and then immediately went back for more, this time going for his throat.

Off to his right a little girl had what looked like a woman of about sixteen on the ground and he stared in shock as the girl ripped open the sixteen year olds stomach and was ripping out intestines and gorging on them like she was eating red licorice. Then she paused, as out of the corner of her eye she saw Henry standing there. She turned to him and with a piece of intestine hanging out of her mouth like a piece of sausage, she advanced on Henry. Henry stood stark still for a moment, his legs didn't want to move; as the girl got closer he could to see the gleam in her eye. Evil, feral, he saw no mercy in those eyes. When she was close enough to try to grab him he snapped out of his fright, he pushed her away and started running away from the fountain, he took one quick look over his shoulder to see if he was being followed and was relieved to see that the girl had lost interest in him and was going for prey closer to her.

Around the girl was complete carnage, the floor of the fountain was stained red with blood as the children gorged themselves on their former parent's bodies. Entrails littered the scene while the children fought over scraps of meat. The screams had just about faded as the parents had been slaughtered and there weren't many vocal chords left intact to scream from.

Other people in the park had started running over to the carnage to see what was wrong. One woman who looked to be out jogging had ran to the edge of the fountain and was calling for help on her cell phone when two kids came at her from behind; she had time for one startled yelp and was thrown to the ground. When she hit the ground three more kids jumped on her ripping and clawing at her face and eyes. Henry heard one muffled scream as she writhed and twitch under the kids, and then she stopped moving.

That was enough for Henry; he turned and ran as fast as could, the fear in his stomach feeling like it was going to explode out of him.

As he rounded a bend on the path he came up to a small drinking fountain, at first it seemed safe but when he got a little closer he saw an older couple lying on the ground next to the fountain. He approached cautiously, there were no signs of trauma and they didn't seem to be moving. He was hesitant about walking by them as there wasn't much room to get by on this part of the path due to boulders on one side and a tight weave of trees and foliage on the other.

He heard sounds behind him and knew he couldn't stay where he was so he cautiously started to creep by the couple. When he had just about made it by them there eyes snapped open, like a puppet on a string they raised themselves to their feet. The old woman jumped on Henry's back as he went by, knocking him to the ground. Before he hit the ground he was able to turn so the old woman was facing him. Her breath was is in his face, it was a mixture of denture cream and death, as she went for his throat he was able to get his hand under her chin and pushed her mouth away from his throat. Her hands were waving in the air as she flailed on top of him. Then out of the corner of his eye he saw the old man crawling over to them. He knew he wouldn't be able to fend them both off at the same time, whether they were old and frail or not. He knew he had to get rid of the woman fast and get the hell out off there. His other hand started fumbling around next to him trying to find some kind of weapon, while his other hand kept her face away from his throat.

Then to his shock or surprise (take your pick) the old woman's dentures fell out and bumped his nose as they fell to the ground. The spittle was coming out of her mouth in what seemed like buckets. It was going into his eyes and mouth and he could feel his stomach wanting to heave as the spittle slid down his throat. Just before the old man reached them he wrapped his hand around a rock.

Henry grabbed it and with all his might slammed it into the side of her head.

There was a sharp crack as it connected; she paused for a moment as if dazed so Henry whacked her again. This time it was a more meaty sound and he could see white through her gray hair, he hit her one more time and this time she stopped fighting him and went limp. He pushed her off him and into the path of the old man and with the extra second it took for the man to crawl over his wife Henry was able to crawl backwards and get to his feet.

Immediately he started wiping the spittle from his face. He was way too grossed out by it to leave it there. Then he turned and got out of there.

When he started running this time he didn't stop until he reached the end of the park.

Thinking he was safe and that the park was an isolated incident his jaw dropped as he got his first look at Main St.

When he had parked his car and walked into the park earlier in the day Main St. had been a peaceful little street with people going about their day with a smile on their face. Storefronts had been filled with window shoppers and bargain hunters.

It was a picture perfect small town street suitable for a postcard.

Now as he stood at the edge of the park and looked onward at the street spread out before him the street definitely did not look the way he had left it.

CHAPTER 8

DR. MARTIN PUT the grounds in the coffee filter and went to the sink with the glass pot to fill it up with water and make another pot of coffee. As the pot filled up he didn't notice the water had a green tint to it as he was doing calculations in his head and really wasn't focusing on the task at hand.

After he poured the water into the machine he went back to his desk to continue comparing the morning results from the afternoons. The bacteria in some of the tanks were showing real progress at destroying the pollution that he had added to them. Each tank had a different substance added, everything from human waste to decomposing bodies, to gasoline.

When he finally succeeded in getting the balance right, the world would finally be able to clean up its polluted harbors and bays.

Just think, an oil tanker spills thousands of gallons of oil into the sea and all they have to do is drop his "patented" bacteria into the spill and BAM; no more spill.

He'd be a hero, hey; maybe he'd even receive the Nobel peace prize, not to mention the financial benefits. All these things were floating around in his head as reached for the pot of coffee.

He took a sip and winced, "Yuck" he said "Needs more sugar." And then took another few sips.

As he was reaching for the sugar he started to feel a little dizzy. He made it back to his desk and sat down, thinking to himself that he'd been working to hard. Then the room started to spin and he felt himself beginning to pass out. The last thing he thought before the darkness took him was where did he put the sugar?

A minute later the former Dr. Martin opened his eyes, he looked around the room, his eyes pausing at the door. Although the living Dr. Martin had an IQ in the high 160s the dead Dr. Martin was running on instinct. The brain functioned but the wiring was all wrong now. He was like an animal now.

He had one desire that overrode any other: hunger.

The former Dr. Martin stumbled to the door, opened it and entered the hallway looking for prey.

CHAPTER 9

JIMMY WAS HIDING out in the break room watching the television when a news bulletin came on.

The reporter was going on about some kind of mass hysteria where people were going crazy and attacking other people. Like most nineteen year olds Jimmy's age he barely paid attention, the last thing he heard before he changed the channel was the reporter urging people to please stay in their homes until the crisis was over. Then the channel jumped to one of those daytime talk shows where everyone cheats on everybody else. He was about to change the channel when he saw Dr. Martin walk by.

"Oh shit," he mumbled to himself. "Dr. Martin figured out what happened earlier and he's coming to fire me."

Dr. Martin stumbled into the room, his mouth was hanging open and a gargling sound was coming from his throat.

"Dude," Jimmy said, "You don't look too hot, are you all right."

Jimmy was about to help him to a chair when for no reason Dr. Martin lunged for his throat, at the last second Jimmy flinched away and the dead man's jaws bit empty air. Jimmy was astonished; this guy was trying to eat him!

"Whoa!" Jimmy screamed, "What the fuck is your problem, man?"

Dr. Martin didn't answer; he just lunged at Jimmy again, his arms flailing in front of him as he advanced on him.

Jimmy picked up a chair and threw it at him and then dodged for the door and ran out into the corridor, when he got to the end of the hall he slammed to a halt. The double metal security doors were in front of him and he had forgotten his security card, remembering it was on the table in the break room. Behind him he heard footsteps as Dr. Martin continued to follow him.

He was trapped; there were no other doors between him and the break room.

He turned back to the door and started banging for help, unfortunately it was getting late in the day and there weren't too many people left around. He turned to face Martin who was about ten feet away and closing fast. He was just trying to prepare himself for a run back down the hallway when he heard the door open behind him. One of Dr. Martin's interns walked in, oblivious to what was going on in front of him. Jimmy pushed him aside and jumped through the door. Before Jimmy could even tell him to close the door Dr. Martin's hand had reached through the partially opened door and pulled the intern back into the hallway with him.

Jimmy got up and ran for the door and pushed it shut, in that fraction of a second as the door slammed shut Jimmy saw Dr. Martin on top of the intern with what looked like his tongue in his mouth. The intern tried to scream while drowning in his own blood but nothing came out but gargling noises.

After that Jimmy could only here shuffling and loud slurping noises on the other side of the door.

As he leaned against the door he remembered that news bite from the television about hysteria and decided it was time to clock out and get the hell out of there.

CHAPTER 10

MARY HAD JUST clocked out for the day and was heading home; she had always enjoyed the drive home. The ride from Pineridge was always peaceful, the one mile winding road that brought her to the highway always quiet.

A couple hundred yards before the road joined the highway Mary spotted a telephone repair truck. As she approached it she noticed no one seemed to be around. The cherry picker part of the truck was at the top of the telephone pole but there was no one in it. Although it seemed odd she didn't really give it much thought. As she was about to pass by the truck a man shuffled out from the front of the truck into the middle of the road. Mary swerved to avoid him and drove off the road, her car getting stuck in the mud. She was about to get out and give that careless man a piece of her mind when he started banging on her window. As she turned to look out the window to yell at him her voice froze in her throat. The man at her window had a screwdriver going into one side of his neck and sticking out the other side.

His hand reached through the partially opened window and grabbed a hunk of her hair. She immediately started trying to resist him but he was just too strong as he pulled her head closer to the window. Her right hand reached for her purse, she grabbed the strap and pulled it to her. When she had a good grip on it she dumped out the contents onto the seat and into her lap. Her eyes searching quickly she found what she wanted and was able to grab it while her head was being shaken around like a fox with a dead chicken in its mouth.

Holding up the small bottle she pressed the top and aimed it in the general direction of the man's face. She new she had hit him when his grip loosened a little, enough so that she was able to pull free while only leaving a little bit of her hair in the mans' hand.

When her mother had given her the bottle of mace she had laughed telling her:

"Mom I live in a quiet little town. Why would I ever need it?"

Mary slid over to the passenger door and fell out of the car, as she pulled herself up the man was just coming around the other side. She started running back to Pineridge when she tripped over a tree root that had been hidden by some leaves left over from the last fall season.

By the time she had regained her footing he had caught up to her again, she started back pedaling back across the road, crab walking backward with her butt dragging on the ground.

Despite everything that was happening and even though she was scared shit she couldn't help thinking "Great, I'm never going to get the stains out of this outfit."

Suddenly a car came screaming around the bend in the road, Mary had just made it to the other side of the road and the zombie was smack dab in the middle. It turned to face the car.

The car hit the man straight on. The zombie bounced of the hood and flew twenty feet into the air hitting the back of the repair truck. Its stomach blew out as it was skewered onto the tools that were hanging on the back of the truck.

Blood and guts exploded onto the dirt in front of it, pooling on the ground.

The man was now pinned to the truck and just flopped around trying to get down, while its intestines continued pouring out. The zombie was able to grab a piece of intestine and noisily started chewing it. The crazy thing was that when it swallowed a piece of meat, a second later it would fall out of the hole in its gut and fall to the ground. Not that it seemed to mind.

Mary just stood at the side of the road, staring at the man who had just attacked her. Not comprehending why he was still alive.

The cars backup lights flashed on and when the car was even with Mary the door opened.

"Mary, you all right?" Jimmy asked her.

She nodded yes and said: "Thanks to you. What the hell is going on?"

"Get in, I'll fill you in on the road, there may be more of those things around."

"You mean there are more people like that out here?" She said as she pointed to the zombie.

"Yeah, I think so."

Mary stumbled over to the car, still a little shaky by her ordeal and climbed into the passenger seat.

"Where are we going Jimmy?" She asked him.

"I'm not sure, but at the moment anywhere's better than here."

Jimmy slammed the car into drive and drove off onto the highway, spraying dirt and dust at the hanging zombie. It didn't seem to care as it happily continued to devour itself piece by piece.

As the car headed down the highway back into town Jimmy didn't realize how wrong his last statement was.

CHAPTER 11

HENRY STOOD AT the entrance to the park on Main St. The street had erupted into panicked chaos, everywhere he looked there were scenes of carnage and death. Across the street he saw a police car; the officer was hanging out of the drivers side window with his neck ripped out, the blood pooling on the ground below him. Henry ran over to the squad car and looked inside. Sure enough, the man still had his gun strapped in its holster.

The poor bastard never even got his police issue Glock out.

Henry moved around to the passenger side door and climbed in, quickly he undid the gun belt and transferred it to his own waist; he was just about to go when he spotted another holster just sticking out of the officer's right pant leg. He reached down and grabbed that one too.

He checked it before he put it in his pocket, it was a Seecamp 32, a backup pistol to the cop but to Henry hopefully salvation. Before he left the car he grabbed the nightstick that was wedged between the seats.

The second he left the car the zombies were on him, he clubbed one in the head and kicked another in the groin, although it had know real effect the zombie did back step once or twice. That was enough of a hole for him to break through, and he took off as fast as he could; weaving in and around them. Though there were a lot of them they didn't move that fast. Hopefully that would be the edge he needed to stay alive. As he turned left down Main St. he saw what was left of his car. A tanker truck had lost control and had crashed taking out his car and a couple of others. Steam was leaking out of the hood of the cab and he could see gasoline pooling under one of the cars, probably due to a ruptured fuel line, he thought.

There were about twenty of the zombies milling about. A few were occupied with their victims. There faces and arms covered in blood and gore.

A woman ran out of a small diner on his left, screaming at the top of her lungs. Moments later a crowd of zombies piled out of the door she had just vacated.

The woman didn't make it more than ten feet before she was overwhelmed by the zombies already on the street. Henry watched helplessly as she was torn apart. Zombies had hold of her from each appendage and were slowly tearing her apart like a starving man devouring a cooked chicken.

The woman's screamed reached a crescendo and then abruptly stopped as her head was torn from her shoulders.

Henry looked away, the anger building in him at his inability to do anything about what he had just witnessed.

He surveyed the street in front of him trying to devise a plan of escape.

The only practical way out of town and the most direct route to his home was past the zombies in the middle of the street. If he tried to run they'd be on him, he knew he didn't have enough bullets for them all and besides he really wasn't a very good shot. The few times he went to the range with a couple of buddies he always did so bad that they would give him shit all the way back home.

Then an idea hit him, he reached inside his pocket for his Zippo lighter. He didn't smoke anymore but he still carried it out of force of habit. He backed up and hid behind a car in the middle of the street, the driver god knows where, and flicked the lighter, when he had a stable flame he tossed it into the pooling gas and ducked down behind the car.

The explosion was so big it nearly tipped the car he was hiding behind on top of him, not only did the cars go up but the tanker truck—luckily not carrying a full fuel load—went up as well. The zombies standing nearest to the blast were immediately incinerated while the ones that were on the outskirts of the blast were thrown to the ground with parts of their bodies on fire.

One zombie was lifted six feet in the air and thrown across the street where he was then impaled onto a parking meter. As it slipped down to the ground it kept squirming, not understanding why it couldn't escape its predicament.

The smell of charred meat filled the street, sickly sweet as it mixed with the smell of burning gas. He was also stunned for a few moments.

When he felt he had his bearings he stood up. His ears were ringing from the blast and so hadn't noticed a group of zombies stumbling towards him from behind, attracted to the area by the sound of the explosion.

When the group was about twenty feet away he turned around and spotted them.

"Oh shit," he breathed. "I am so screwed."

He fumbled at his waist for the holster and got the Glock out, He tried to relax, breathe slow, exhale and then squeeze the trigger.

The first bullet hit one of the zombies in the chest, the exit wound blowing a fist size chunk out of its back. Blood and guts sprayed the zombie behind it, although it didn't seem to care. The second round caught a fat bald zombie right in the left eye, as the back of his head disintegrated he dropped like a bag of potatoes.

"Well I'll be," he said, "just like in the fuckin' movies."

Off to his side he saw a zombie climb out of a green jeep. Henry noticed the license plate said veteran on it. As the gray haired zombie started to stumble his way he calmly turned the gun at it and put a bullet right between its eyes.

"Sorry buddy," he said as he turned to face the next threat.

Henry stared at his handiwork for a moment and thanked God he was becoming a better marksman.

After that he disposed of them rather quickly. When a woman zombie had its head turned sideways he managed to put one right in her ear, the bullet bouncing around in her skull before exiting out the side of her face and taking off half her jaw with it, her waitress uniform was drenched in her own blood.

Her name tag, which read "Hi I'm Wendy," was covered in her blood to the point of illegibility as she slumped to the ground.

After taking the rest of the zombies in his immediate area out of action he checked Main St. one more time and started running down the street and avoiding the fires.

Some of store fronts were really starting to burn. As he ran by he wondered if there'd be anyone left to put them out.

He'd have a two mile walk ahead of him before he'd arrive home; he hoped Emily was all right. She must be worried, he thought.

As he was walking down the highway he smiled to himself, he was glad he had got that nap in. Thinking back to when he had been on that park bench he would never have imagined how much he would need it.

CHAPTER 12

THE OLD DELTA 88 cruised down the highway heading into town; the radio newscaster was talking about some kind of epidemic, the officials saying that somehow the town's water had been contaminated and at all costs avoid coming into contact with it.

"You see Jimmy, I told you, I mean I never thought it was this extreme but if you hadn't had that bottle of water with me you'd be infected too."

"Christ Mary, I still think that's horse shit but, seeing is believing," Jimmy smirked.

"So what do we do now?" Mary asked. "Do we try to get out of town?"

"First, I'd like to see for myself if it's as bad as they say, if it is then yes, we'll head for the hills; so to speak."

They hadn't seen anyone since Jimmy had picked her up and they were starting to relax a little when they saw another zombie walking on the side of the road. It was dragging a dog leash behind him, although there was no dog to be seen.

"Watch this," Jimmy said with a devilish smirk on his face.

The Delta picked up speed and just when Mary thought he was just going to drive by it, he swerved into it and struck it right at the knees.

The zombie flew over the hood of the car, its head cracking the windshield on its way to the ground. There was a red smudge on the glass left over from its passage. It landed in a heap; its legs bent up to its body like a V. To Mary's surprise it was still moving, as it tried to drag itself after them with one arm, the other limb was a splintered mess of bone and tissue. In fact she could also see pieces of its shin poking through the skin of its legs.

She turned away disgusted. Jimmy stared with boyhood glee, feeling safe inside his tank on wheels.

"Holy shit it's still kickin'. Well fuck, I'll take care of that." He said smiling at Mary.

"You're sick Jimmy," she glared back.

Jimmy put the car in reverse and picked up speed. His back tire ran over the zombie's head dead center. There was a loud pop and for a moment Jimmy thought he might have blown a tire but as the car completely rolled over the corpse he could see that the head was crushed flat, with brain matter all over the road.

Feeling good about a job well done he put the car in drive and continued down the highway; the brains in the treads of the tire flying off into the shoulder of the road.

A mile down the road they came upon a parked car on the shoulder of the road.

Jimmy slowed down to investigate, wondering if someone needed help.

As he pulled up behind the car he turned to Mary and said: "Stay here, I'll be right back. Roll the windows up just in case."

Then Jimmy stepped out of his car and walked over to the parked car.

As he moved closer he saw something for just a second in the back seat and then it disappeared just as quick. Jimmy looked around on the ground and spotted a fist sized rock. Bending over to retrieve it he weighed it in his hand.

"Better than nothing." He muttered to himself as he slowly approached the car.

When he was even with the windows he looked inside and immediately jumped back with a yell.

"Holy shit, there are people in there." He called to Mary.

Mary rolled her window down and called to him.

"Really, are they all right?"

Ahh," Jimmy hesitated, "Not exactly."

Mary decided it was safe enough to get out and see for her self. Climbing out of the passenger door she walked along the shoulder and stopped next to Jimmy.

When she was beside him she followed his gaze into the car to see what he had meant.

She looked inside the car and then immediately turned and vomited onto the shoulder.

Jimmy jumped back so he wouldn't get sprayed as he yelled at her.

"Jesus Mary, didn't I tell you to stay in the god damn car?"

Mary wiped her mouth with her sleeve and apologized. "Sorry Jimmy, I just wanted to see what was going on."

"And are you glad you did?" He asked her.

"Definitely not, I would have been just fine if I hadn't."

She looked back into the car and this time she was ready and was able to keep from vomiting again. She turned to Jimmy. "You're going to do something about it aren't you?" The look in her eyes was judging him and it made him capitulate to her demands easily.

Turning, Jimmy walked back to his car and popped the trunk, reaching inside to retrieve something Mary couldn't see.

When he closed the trunk and walked back to her she could see he had a tire iron in his hand hanging by his side.

He looked at her and waved her away so he had room to open the car's door.

Then he opened the door and got to work.

CHAPTER 13

WHEN JIMMY THREW open the car door he was immediately assaulted by the smell. He started to breathe through his mouth to try to keep from gagging as he felt his stomach getting ready to heave.

There were three people in the car, or to put it better, there was one person in the car and the remains of two others.

When Jimmy threw the door open a women looked up from the backseat where she had attacked and killed her two children. In the backseat in two booster seats were the remains of a boy and girl. Their ages were somewhere between eight and ten. It was hard for Jimmy to tell as there wasn't much left of their faces.

When the mother had swung into a local convenient store to grab a cup of coffee and get her kids each an ice cream sundae she had no idea she would be signing their death certificates. But she had wanted a fresh cup of coffee that was just brewed. Unfortunately it came from the water supply that was supplied from the pipes inside the walls.

The older pot that had sat on the burner had been made before the water had been contaminated and would have been fine. But fate had decided different.

After Mom had taken a few sips of her coffee after leaving the store she had started feeling dizzy and had pulled over to rest. The last thing she heard before the blackness of death took her was of her kids calling her name from the backseat; asking if she was all right.

When Mom woke up again she felt an irresistible hunger; she was ravenous in her need to quench it.

Then she heard voices in the backseat. Turning around she saw fresh meat.

And best of all it was strapped in and couldn't run. As she turned and climbed over the seat to begin feeding a tiny part of her old self screamed in horror at what her body was about to do.

As the screams started inside the car a flock of birds took flight from the trees overhead, flying off to quieter pastures; the screams of the two children continued long into the day.

Mom hissed at Jimmy, upset that she had been disturbed. Jimmy put his hand over his nose to try to cut down on the smell as he whacked the door window with the crowbar.

The window shattered spraying the mother and kids with safety glass.

Jimmy was trying to get her to leave the car so he would be able to whack her in the head with the crowbar.

Mom hissed again but wouldn't leave.

Jimmy swore under his breathe, why did it always have to be hard? He thought.

These things are all over the place trying to eat me and I have to find the one that's not interested. He frowned as he tried to think of another way to get it out of the car.

Then he walked as close as he dared and stuck his leg at the zombie and pulled his pant leg up.

"Come on honey, come and get it. Mmmm, white meat." He said as he shook his leg at the zombie.

Mom hesitated for a minute and then started to creep out of the car. As she crawled over her dead children she slipped on the blood covering the seat and landed on her face in the dirt.

That's when Jimmy brought the crowbar down on her head as hard as he could manage.

But he rushed the blow and just grazed her skull.

Instead of caving her head in he just ripped her scalp open and tore some of her hair off.

Mom started crawling after Jimmy quicker than he expected and he stumbled back out of her reach until he was at the back of the car.

Mom was moving pretty quick for a zombie and Jimmy couldn't get a killing blow in, as a matter of fact he was working hard at just keeping her off of him. As the two of them went back and forth behind the car Jimmy started to panic that this wasn't going to work out quite the way he had hoped, when all of a sudden he heard the Delta's engine rev and then the horn shrieked behind him.

Jimmy turned around to see Mary behind the wheel coming straight at him. He dived out of the way and landed in the road as Mary continued forward.

Mary plowed the car straight into the other one and caught the zombie in the middle.

The zombies waist shattered as the two cars connected and she fell across the hood of the car. Mary then backed up a little allowing the zombie to slip off of the hood and come to a sitting position behind the parked car; with her head leaning against the bumper. Mary then slammed the car back into drive and surged forward.

The zombies head was crushed between the two bumpers and exploded into the cars grill. The brains now steaming on the radiator as Mary backed the car free from the other car's bumper.

Jimmy just sat on the road in awe as Mary leaned out the window and looked at him.

"Never send a man to do a women's job." She smiled at him.

Jimmy stood up a little embarrassed and brushed himself off.

"I got nothin'," he said with his hands out in front of him and then he walked back to the car and hopped in.

Mary put the car in drive and they continued on down the highway.

"The first chance we get pull over, I'm driving." He said from the passenger seat.

"Sure Jimmy, no problem," Mary said, stroking his ego. "You did great, you set her up and I took her down." She said as the wind blew her hair around her head.

Jimmy looked at her askance and smiled. "Yeah, I guess I did. We make a pretty good team."

She smiled back. "Jimmy my dear, I believe we do."

Later after they had changed seats and Jimmy was driving again he spotted another zombie on the opposite side of the road coming from town. He was just starting to speed up and swerve into the other lane when it put up its hands and started waving them back and forth.

Jimmy slowed down and was a little surprised when he realized he recognized this man.

"Holy shit," Jimmy said with a surprised look on his face. "I know that guy."

"Really, who is it?" Mary questioned him.

"That's old man Watson; he lives a couple of houses down the street from me. My Dad knows him better than I do; I used to cut his grass when I was I was a kid."

Jimmy slowed down and pulled over next to Henry.

"Hey Mr. Watson, I almost thought you were a zombie," Jimmy smiled at him.

"Jimmy, wow, thank god someone else is still alive, I haven't seen anyone since I left town you're the first people I've seen."

"Yeah, same for us, where are you going?"

"I'm heading home to get my wife and get the hell out of this town. Where are you going? If you're thinking of going into town you can forget it. The towns a mess, those damn things are everywhere."

"No shit I was hoping it wasn't as bad as the news said it was, fuck we're low on gas and I don't really know what to do now. I'm kind of new at this doomsday shit."

Would you give me a ride back home?" Henry asked. "Once I grab Emily we can all take her minivan and go. I know it's got gas, I just filled it up yesterday."

"Sure Mr. Watson hop in."

Before Henry got in he noticed the front of the car and with raised eyebrows asked Jimmy about it.

"You kids get into any trouble?" He asked with a grin.

"Nothing we couldn't handle, old man, now come on, get in, times wastin'. By the way this is Mary." Jimmy said as he turned the car around and drove back the way they had come. At least now they had a destination.

"Hi Mary, nice to meet you and please both of you, call me Henry." He said with a smile on his face.

"Sure Henry," Mary smiled back.

Ten minutes later they pulled in front of Henry's house, the neighborhood was eerily quiet. If Henry didn't know any better he would have thought it was Sunday morning.

"Stay sharp," Henry whispered. "There're probably a few around here depending on how many people drank the tap water today."

No sooner did he finish then he saw his neighbor come walking out of his garage, his face was covered in blood and he was munching on something unidentifiable. When he saw the three of them he hissed and started walking at them faster.

Henry calmly pulled his Glock out and waited for the zombie to get a little closer, then before he pulled the trigger he yelled: "You know what, I never really liked you Charlie!" and then put a bullet right between his eyes.

The zombie slumped to the ground and didn't stir again.

"I'm going inside, here take this," Henry said as he handed the Seecamp to Jimmy." Just point and shoot, head shots only or they won't go down. Keep watch out here and yell if there's a problem. I'll only be a couple of minutes."

With that done Henry pulled out his house keys and proceeded to enter his house.

CHAPTER 14

THE HOUSE WAS quiet. As Henry entered the house through the back door the first thing he was aware of was the kitchen television. He could hear it down the hall as he walked into the kitchen looking for Emily. The first thing he saw upon entering the room was Emily sitting at the kitchen table. She was slumped over something on the table and was so involved with it that she hadn't noticed Henry enter the room.

On closer inspection Henry noticed a cup with a teabag had fallen onto the floor by her feet and had shattered into a hundred tiny fragments, the shards reflecting the light off the television and the kitchen light, which was turned down low.

Henry walked up behind her, he was hesitant to say anything as after all the shit that had already gone down today, and he really didn't know how to start. Saying something like, "HI, honey I'm home, boy you wouldn't believe the day I've had. I've been running all over town today killing zombies and boy am I hungry. What's for supper? And oh yeah I brought company home to." Just didn't sound right.

Before he had a chance to decide what he was going to do his right shoe stepped on some of the fragments from the tea cup. To Henry the sound it made sounded like a firecracker going off although in reality it was barely audible. Either way it was enough to alert Emily that there was another presence in the room.

She turned slowly around, her bathrobe falling open as she faced him, she was nude under her robe and as she looked up at Henry she smiled, but not her "Hi honey how was your day?" smile.

No this smile said "Hi, honey I'd like to kill you." Her teeth were blood red as her head turned to look at him.

As she turned in the chair he was now able to see what had had her so preoccupied when he had entered the room. Their cat "Romero" was laying on the table with what was left of his insides hanging out, his fur was matted with blood and his mouth was hanging open.

Emily rose from the table and walked straight for him, hands reaching out, while her teeth gnashed up and down. Henry backpedaled, for the moment too shocked to act, his back coming up against the stove, trapping him. She plowed into him; he felt a sharp pain in his back. The handles to the oven door had gouged into his back. By instinct alone he pushed her away sending her flying across the kitchen and crashing into the microwave cart at the other end of the room. Henry took a deep breathe and collected himself.

God help him he knew what he had to do.

While Emily regained her feet he reached around behind him. His hand wrapped around the handle to the cast iron skillet sitting on top of the stove.

When she was in arms reach he swung it as hard as he could. An image of a baseball bat connecting with a home run ball flashed through his mind.

The skillet connected with the side of her head with a clang, Henry felt the impact right up through his shoulder. Emily went down; blood flowing from her head wound, the red liquid dripping down over her breasts. Henry straddled her lifting the pan over his head and with both hands he closed his eyes and with all his might brought the pan down on top of her face. Emily's nose disintegrated under the force of the blow, bone fragments from her nose pushing into her brain.

Henry didn't notice. With his eyes closed and a silent scream in his throat he continued to bring the pan down onto her head.

When he finally stopped and opened his eyes, there was nothing left of her head but deflated skin surrounded by a puddle of blood, brain matter covered the kitchen cabinets leaving thin bloody snail trails down the doors as gravity took over.

Henry stood up and backed away from her, twenty years they'd been married, and despite all the bullshit two people deal with in life he still loved her as much as the first day they were married. The kitchen wall stopped his backwards progress; he slumped to the floor, put his head down, and cried.

He continued to cry until he heard a woman's scream and gunshots coming from outside the house.

CHAPTER 15

JIMMY WATCHED HENRY enter the house. As he leaned on the car with Mary at his side he couldn't help noticing how quiet the street was. Usually the street would be full of the sounds of life. Cars going by, lawnmowers cutting grass, and kids playing in yards, today it was quiet," Too quiet" as they would always say in the movies. He caught something out of the corner of his eye but when he turned to look at it straight on it had disappeared. He shrugged figuring it was a trick of the light.

Mary had caught a slight glimpse too but unlike Jimmy didn't shrug it off as a fluke.

She walked over to where she last saw it. There were some hedges about three feet tall surrounding the property line of the house next door; the shrubs were manicured to resemble a green fence. When she was within earshot of the shrubs she could hear small slurping sounds. The sounds grew louder as she walked closer. When she was close enough to peek over the hedges she stopped.

Horrified beyond belief she stared at the scene in front of her for a second. Then she slowly backed away.

When she got back to the car Jimmy could see something was wrong.

"What's up Mary, you see something?" He asked.

She just pointed to the hedges and then vomited onto the grass.

Jimmy pushed himself off the car and walked over to the hedges, the slurping sounds could now be heard by him as well. He also heard another sound as well, buzzing, a lot of it.

There was a woman lying behind the shrubs, she was wearing what looked like a maternity shirt and one of those summer beverage pitchers,—the ones with watermelons or lemons painted on them—was lying on the ground next to her.

He also noticed a book lying by her head, the title reading something about baby names.

Her face looked peaceful, as if she'd just lain down for a nap. That wasn't what had freaked Mary out.

Jimmy could only see this much of her as the hedges were still blocking the rest of her body. As he walked right up to the hedges he was able to look down and see one of the most gruesome scenes he had ever seen in his life.

From the chest down the woman was a bloody mess, flies were everywhere, and in the middle of her abdomen sat a small child no more than a few days old, the child was on all fours like a dog with its head buried deep into her body. The slurping sounds were mixed with ripping sounds as the baby ripped organs and tissue from its mothers' body, the umbilical chord moving back and forth with the baby's movements.

Jimmy spotted a baseball bat and glove laying a little ways in the yard. He retrieved the bat and went back to the body. With a firm two-handed grip he swung the bat at the baby. The bat hit with such force the baby zombie's head almost ripped from its shoulders. A few muscles and skin the only thing preventing the head from falling off. The zombies' eyes continued to blink at Jimmy, the toothless mouth moving up and down.

With one more swing he severed the head from the neck sending it flying across the lawn. It rolled twice then lay still. There was a picnic blanket near the woman's body, Jimmy grabbed it and spread it over her, silently saying a prayer.

Then walked over to the severed head and kicked it into the bushes.

He breathed a sigh of relief that it was over and turned to go back to Mary.

That's when Mary began to scream.

CHAPTER 16

WHEN MARY SCREAMED Jimmy looked up from the woman's corpse to see Mary backing away from two zombies who had come up on them unobserved by stumbling through Henry's backyard. One of the walking corpses was carrying something that looked an awful lot like raw liver.

Jimmy grabbed the bat and started running towards her, when he was close enough he swung the bat at the first zombie sending it off balance, the second one he hit with his shoulder pushing it to the ground. As it landed the zombie's hairpiece flew of and landed to the side of him.

"Run to the house I'll slow these guys down." He yelled at her turning to the first zombie again.

The first one was up again and the second one was crawling towards him as he backed up to give himself some breathing room. Then he remembered the gun in his pocket from Mr. Watson. He pulled it out and aimed it at the first one. The gun bucked in his hand as the bullet hit the zombie in the side of the neck. Blood flew from the wound, spraying Jimmy in the face and going into his eyes. He couldn't see! As he brought his sleeve up to wipe his face the second zombie had crawled close enough to him to get its hands around his boot. Jimmy tried backing up to get away from baldie but instead lost his balance.

Falling to the ground he whacked the back of his head on the pavement. Flashes of light flew across his vision for a second. He blinked his eyes closed a few times as his vision became clearer. When his eyes focused he saw the face of baldie coming down to take a bite out of him. He raised the Seecamp up and jammed it in the zombie's mouth, squeezing the trigger as it bit down on the gun. There was a muffled pop and the zombie went still, lying on top of Jimmy.

Jimmy couldn't move. His gun was trapped between baldie and himself.

Baldie was stretched out on top of him and the dead weight of the body was weighing him down! The other zombie was down by his feet and as Jimmy tried to kick it in the face it latched on to his boot with both hands. The zombie was about to make a McJimmy out of him. He tried to kick it off but its grip was too damn tight.

He closed his eyes bracing himself for the pain that was to come when he heard a wet thwack. And at the same time felt the zombie let go of his leg. He opened his eyes to see Mary standing over him. She had a smile on her face as she leaned over to help pull him out from under the body. He saw the baseball bat lying next to her where she'd dropped it after cold cocking the zombie in the head. As she helped him up they could both see the street was filling up with zombies. Attracted by all the noise they'd been making, the houses around them were disgorging zombies looking for new prey.

"Go to the house, I'm right behind you." Jimmy breathed as he bent over to pick up the gun, as an afterthought he retrieved the bat too. So far it had come in handy.

Running to the house he took a few pot shots at some of the zombies who were closer than some of the others. Some of the bullets hit the bodies, but didn't slow them down, and then the gun dry clicked. He was out of bullets. Taking one more look around he turned and headed into the house after Mary with the zombies close on their heels.

CHAPTER 17

THE SECOND JIMMY got inside the house and locked the door behind him he knew something wasn't right in the house. Mary was just standing in the entrance to the kitchen and Henry was across the room sitting on the floor. As he pushed by Mary to enter the room he saw what the problem was. A woman was on the floor with her head bashed in. Even though he felt stupid for asking he walked over and bent down near Henry.

"Was that your wife Mr. Watson?" Jimmy asked quietly.

"I had to kill her, she was one of them, she attacked me." He replied to no one in particular.

"That's okay Henry, you had no choice." Jimmy turned to Mary.

"Help me get him up, we'll put him in the living room," he grunted while picking up Henry.

Mary went over and grabbed his other arm and together they half walked, half carried him into the living room. Once there they set him on the couch. Henry rolled over on to his side and started crying again softly.

Jimmy motioned Mary to follow him and together they went back to the kitchen.

"Henry said there's a minivan in the garage, you find the keys and I'll get rid of the body," said Jimmy bending over and grabbing Emily by the legs and dragging her to the back door.

Mary went off into the other rooms searching for the keys.

Jimmy took a peak out of one of the back windows, the zombies were just wandering around aimlessly, with no apparent purpose, for the moment forgetting about them inside the house.

When the back yard looked clear he opened the door and quickly dragged the body outside. Dropping it in the dirt, he turned and ran back inside slamming the door shut behind him. As soon as he slammed the lock back into place he heard a thump on the other side of the door. One of the zombies had seen him and now knew they were trying to get in the house. Soon others were wandering over attracted to the noise of the other one.

Mary came back jingling keys in her left hand, "Look what I found, I also found a couple of cases of bottled water in the pantry." she said apparently satisfied with herself.

"Emily used to always tease me about drinking bottled water when it was free from the tap."

Henry was standing in the front entrance to the kitchen." Sorry about before, I guess this day finally caught up to me," He looked down to the floor, and muttered," And now Emily . . . ."

"Look we really don't have time for this, those things know were in here, and there's no way we can fight off the amount that are out there. We need a plan." Jimmy said.

Henry seemed to shake his stupor off as he became more focused.

"Agreed, I think we should load up the van with food and water and try to get to the city limits, if whatever is going on in this town is local then we need to get out of the effected area fast."

Henry looked at Mary and asked, "Mary would you get those cases of water and put them by the door leading to the garage?"

"Sure Henry, anything else?" Mary inquired.

"Yeah grab what canned goods you can as well."

"Jimmy, do you still have the gun I gave you?" Henry asked.

"Yeah but its empty, I emptied it trying to get in here."

"Shit, I've only got about half a clip left. We need to find more guns or we're never gonna make it out of this shit." He grunted.

Just then the two back windows broke, glass falling everywhere. Luckily the house sat high in the back so though the zombies broke the windows all you could see were there hands and wrists flailing in the frame. The glass cut and sliced there hands, blood flowing from wounds that would have killed a live human being in minutes.

Mary came back, breathing a little heavy; she said," All done, what's next?"

Henry looked at her and grinned. "Next is we get the fuck out of here".

CHAPTER 18

TOGETHER THEY QUICKLY loaded the van with food and water. Henry had a couple of old blankets lying around the garage, so he threw them in the van as well.

Jimmy wandered over to the corner of the garage where Henry stored all his yard tools.

"Hey Henry, what about using some of these for weapons," he said while pointing to the tools.

"Sure go for it," Henry huffed while moving boxes around in the back of the van to make more room. "There better than nothing, though I'd rather not have those things so close to me that I had to use them.

Jimmy started grabbing stuff, a few looked promising. Hanging up on a peg board was an old pair of hedge clippers, he took them down and opened and closed them a few times.

"Nice," he murmured to himself. He also grabbed a pitchfork and an old worn shovel with curved sides that ended in a pointed tip.

"Hey Mary," Henry called out from inside the van, would you go over there with Jimmy and see if any of those paint cans and bottles can be of any use?"

"Yeah sure," she said heading over to Jimmy's side. The shelves were full of what you'd expect to find in a middle class suburban garage. Half full paint cans leftover from finished projects lined the shelves, and then in the back on the top shelf she noticed a whiskey bottle.

"Hey Henry," she called while reaching up to grab the bottle off the shelf," what's this?"

Henry climbed out of the van and blushed a little when he saw what she was holding.

"Oh ah, you know, sometimes you need a little pick-me-up; and Emily didn't like alcohol in the house being that her father had been an alcoholic.

Mary's brow wrinkled in concentration for a second and then she said "Could we make those cocktail thingies with the fire on the end to throw at those things?"

"Molotov Cocktails? Shit Mary, that's a great idea, we'll use those empty bottles behind you and these old rags here," Jimmy said holding up a couple of what looked like old shirts that had served their purpose well and were now being conscripted into rag service.

The three of them got to work filling the empty bottles with some of the whiskey and then ripping the old shirts into wicks and pushing them into the top of the bottles.

Henry grabbed a partially depleted gallon of paint thinner to use as fuel as well.

Then Jimmy got up and went over to the washing machines in the corner and came back with a jug of laundry detergent in his hands and a mischievous grin on his face.

"What are you gonna do with that?" Mary asked, looking up at him from the floor where they had all sat down to make the cocktails.

"I saw it in a movie once; when you add this to those bottles you've got a simple version of napalm."

Henry's eyes widened with understanding, but before he could answer there was a crashing from inside the house. Henry ran back into the house to see what it was.

The front picture window in the living room had been smashed in from the weight of the zombies pressing on it. Although the window was waist high off the ground some of the zombies had been trampled to the ground and other ones were able to use them as step stools to be able to climb inside the house. Henry took it all in at a glance and then headed back to the garage. Detouring by the kitchen he rummaged through one of the kitchen drawers and smiled when he found the object of his search; his spare cigarette lighter.

"We've only got a few minutes before they're in here," Henry said, rushing back into the garage and closing the door behind him. "This door doesn't lock from this side so there's no way to keep those bastards out of here, so as I already said, let's get the fuck out of here."

Jimmy and Mary had just finished modifying the cocktails and had been putting them in an old box. The box was from an old case of bottled beer and was perfect to hold the cocktails.

As Henry ran over to help them load the rest of the stuff into the car the door to the garage started rattling in its frame and then started opening.

The first one through, Henry saw, was actually someone he knew. It was old Ms. McLusky from down the street. Her hair was up in rollers, and her mouth hung open, she had that glassy stare that the creatures all seemed to have when they weren't focused on any one thing.

She was having trouble getting through the door due to the fact that the weight of the other zombies behind her was pressing on the door, and the door opened in. She had gotten halfway through the door and was now trapped between the frame and the door.

Jimmy acted quickly, and while Mary finished loading the van (a little quicker than before) he grabbed the pair of hedge clippers and headed for the zombie.

When he was on top of her he opened the clippers as wide as they would go and when her neck was in-between them, squeezed with all his might.

The two blades came together with a slicing sound, her head falling to the ground, her neck geysered blood all over the garage hitting Henry who was a good four feet away.

He flinched away to avoid the viscous liquid and then ran over to grab Jimmy.

"Come on we've got to go now!" he urged while pulling Jimmy back to the van

With the headless body slumping to the ground the other zombies were managing to wedge the door open a little at a time.

Henry jumped into the driver's seat as the others followed suit, slamming their doors in controlled panic.

A little voice inside Henry wanted to yell at them for slamming the vans doors, but then it fluttered away back to where notions came from. With the situation what it is, the last thing he should care about is the doors to the van.

"Ready?" He asked them with his hand on the garage door opener.

"No," Jimmy said nervously, next to him in the passenger seat, "But go ahead anyway."

Henry hit the button to the opener and as he floored the gas petal to escape the garage he saw in his door mirror on the floor of the garage Ms. McLusky's head where it had landed in the corner. For a moment the head was lost from sight as the other zombies flooded into his garage, and then he could see the old woman's head clearly again.

In that split second glimpse he could swear that it looked right at him and smiled.

CHAPTER 19

SCOTT PETERS PEEKED out the basement window of his one family ranch house. The street was full of walking corpses. At the moment they didn't seem that threatening, but as Scott had seen first hand, if one of them got a hold of you, you were finished.

That's what had happened earlier in the day, when all this craziness had started. He had heeded what the news was telling him. He had avoided the water from the sink and had gathered all the juice, soda, and beer he had in the house and put all of it into the cellar.

Then he waited to see what would happen next. A little at a time he had seen his neighbors coming out of their houses, but they didn't do anything, just stood there staring at nothing.

After awhile a police car had come down the street. When the car had slowed to avoid the people in the street the car had squawked its horn for the people to move. When nothing happened the passenger door opened and a policeman got out. He started waving his arms trying to shoo the people out of the way, asking them to please stand aside.

That's when it happened.

To Scott's horror he watched as the crowd turned on the cop and as one swarmed over him. He barely had time to let out a shout before he was smothered by bodies.

Scott couldn't really see what was happening to the officer as the crowd was too tightly packed, but then as the screams faded from the dying man he saw people moving off from the group with what looked to Scott like pieces of a human body.

A little girl walked over to the curb and sat down, gnawing on what looked like a hand.

Two others had grabbed a leg and were now fighting over it as blood and bits of meat flew everywhere. The driver got out with a look of absolute shock on his face. As the zombies turned to attack him as he started backing away. Pulling his Glock from its holster, Scott heard him yelling at the crowd to back off or he'd shoot. When no one obeyed he opened fire.

From where Scott was standing at his window he could only see the backs of the zombies, when all of a sudden the back of one them exploded spraying blood and gore over the street.

For a second Scott could see the officer on the other side of the zombie through the hole in its body. He could see the look of terror on the man's face.

As the man kept firing he didn't see two more coming at him from his blindside, the zombies hands wrapped around his throat and face and pulled him to the ground. One sank its teeth into his throat ripping it to shreds, as the cop tried to scream another zombies jaw came down over his mouth muffling his screams. To Scott it looked like the zombie was kissing the man, but then as it's head reared back Scott could see something wiggling between its teeth, For a second it didn't register in his mind what it could possibly be. Then it hit him. It was the man's tongue. That was all Scott could take, he ran to the first trash bucket that was near and expelled his breakfast.

When he returned to the window a few moments later the street was relatively quiet. The ten or so zombies in the area just wandered around harmlessly.

There wasn't much left of the two men outside on the ground. Most of the zombies were congregated around them, eating in frenzy, oblivious of their surroundings for the moment. When there was nothing left of the two policemen the zombies started wandering away. Scott watched through the window as the last one departed the area around the police car. Now he was able to see into the squad car. His eyes lit up when he saw what was hanging on the front of the cage on the inside that separates the front and back of the car. A twelve gauge shotgun, and as luck would have it he knew how to use one. Now the only thing was how he was going to get it and get away before those things ripped him to shreds.

About a half hour had passed since the zombies had killed the policemen outside. Scott was on the first floor of his house looking out the front window when he noticed his neighbor in the window across the street.

She was signaling to him. He ran to his closet to retrieve his binoculars and then went back to the window. She had a children's chalkboard in front of the window and as Scott watched she wrote something and then held it up to the window for him to see it.

It said "Husband dead, tried kill me, locked him in bathroom."

Then she took it down and wrote something else and put it back up again.

This time it read "Door won't hold, need leave, come to you?"

Scott took the binoculars down from his eyes and looked at her.

The zombies were still outside and would probably be on her in minutes if she tried to leave the house.

Scott held up his hand and went to find something he could write on. He came up with a piece of cardboard he was using to hold a puzzle he was working on. Grabbing a big black marker he quickly returned to his window; she was still there waiting for him.

Scott wrote on his piece of cardboard and held it up so she could read it, he also wrote big enough so she could see the letters unaided.

He wrote "Risky, Take chance?"

She then started writing again and held the chalkboard up.

It said: "No choice, Bath door break soon."

After Scott read her sign he frowned, the odds of her making it to his house was slim, but if she stayed where she was she would probably die too.

Scott wrote two more words and held them up.

They said "Good luck."

She then held the chalkboard up one last time, the words "5 minutes" printed clearly. Then she disappeared from the window. Scott assuming she was getting ready to make her mad dash to the safety of his house.

Scott stood at the window, the five minutes seeming to take hours. Finally he watched as her door opened and she ran out into the street, she was barefoot and had a rolling pin in her hand as she tried to make it across the street.

Scott could only watch as the zombies started to swarm around her. There were about eight of them on the street at the time she had come out of her house and they stood directly in her path to Scott's house. She managed to dodge the first two as they lunged for her, another she clubbed in the head with the rolling pin.

The zombie didn't go down but it did hesitate enough for her to get around it.

By now she was in the middle of the street and she was being blocked by three more. She was swinging the rolling pin back and forth in front of her, keeping the zombies at bay but her attention was so focused in front of her she didn't see one of the dead come out from behind her hedges and come up on her from behind.

Despite Scott not wanting to alert the zombies he was in his house he banged on the window, trying to get her attention but she couldn't hear him and was much too occupied trying to stay out of the zombies reach.

Within moments the zombie had come up on her and grabbed her, the weight of its body dragging her down. She screamed in defiance as they swarmed over her, her screams of anger soon turning to screams of pain.

Scott just stood there helpless. What could he do? He was unarmed and only one man. If he went out there he would be killed to.

He stood there and watched as she was ripped to pieces. Her body twitched in its death throes for what seemed to Scott for quite a while but finally she lay still.

As the zombies wandered away from her after having their fill Scott could see her torso had been ripped open, the organs inside torn out and devoured.

Her face was locked in a mask of terror; what was left of it anyway.

Through the tears in Scott's eyes he could see that her eyes were missing, the openings nothing more than gaping holes on her face.

To his surprise he saw something sticking out of her mouth. Scott retrieved his binoculars and zoomed in to see what it was.

It was an ear, though his heart was breaking inside at the death of his friend he smiled. She had gone down fighting right to the last second.

Scott could only hope when his time came that he would have as much courage.

CHAPTER 20

THE SUN REFLECTED off the windshield of the minivan as it flew out of the garage, momentarily blinding Henry. The front of the van plowed through the crowd of walking dead, sending them flying in every direction as the van careened out of the driveway and into the street.

One of the zombies was able to grab on to the windshield wipers as the van plowed into it.

"Get that fuckin' thing off the car, Jimmy!" He yelled while trying to maintain control of the wheel.

Jimmy paused, thinking how to do it. He reached over and turned on the wipers, the arms of the wipers jumping back and forth slapping the thing in the face. As blood was pouring out of the zombie's broken nose, the wiper blades began spreading the blood over the windshield severely decreasing Henry's field of vision. Without thinking about it Henry hit the windshield washer fluid button, sending blue fluid into the zombie's mouth. It flinched a little trying to spit the washer fluid back out, blood and washer fluid mixing together to turn the windshield a pale purple color.

Mary sat in the backseat watching the proceedings, though she was scared out of her mind another part of her realized what a ridiculous scene she was seeing.

The van jumped as Henry ran over another walker that was to slow to get out of the way.

Something poked her leg as she bounced around on her seat, while Henry tried to maneuver around all the zombies, she looked down and saw the pitchfork Jimmy had thrown in the van with the other tools he'd found. She picked it up.

"Here try using this," she said while handing him the tool.

"Use this how?" He asked no one in particular.

"Use it to pry it of the damn windshield!" Henry yelled at him.

"Jimmy rolled down the window, and leaned out, it was tough to reach the zombie as it was mostly on Henry's side.

"Slow down a little, I've gotta lean out more and I don't want to fall out," Jimmy yelled back into the van.

"Fine, just hurry the fuck up!" Henry screamed back.

Trying to drive around all the obstacles in the road and having this damn zombie staring at him through the windshield was really freaking him out.

Jimmy leaned out as far as he could go and stuck the pitchfork into its ribs. More blood flew onto the windshield making it even harder for Henry to see; if that was possible.

Jimmy pulled back with all of his might, but the thing just wouldn't let go. Then one of the blades broke off the hood momentarily throwing the zombie off balance. Jimmy took advantage of this and with a yell pulled with everything he had. The zombie popped off the hood, and for a fraction of a second seemed to hang in mid air in front of the van. Then it was lost from view rolling under the minivan. The van jumped like it had hit a speed bump throwing Jimmy off balance. He felt himself falling out the window, the pavement coming up to kiss his face when he was jarred to a halt. Then thank God he felt himself being pulled back in. Just before he got himself all the way back inside the van a zombie was able to grab a handful of his hair. He yelped in pain as a piece of his scalp was ripped off his head. Blood trickled down his neck, pooling around his collar.

Once inside he turned around, where Mary had just sat down again, after grabbing his belt and pulling him back in.

"Shit that was close," he panted. "I thought I was goin' down, Jesus, Mary, it seems like your making a habit out of saving my ass."

"Someone's gotta do it," she smiled back. She leaned over to take a look at his head.

"It doesn't look too bad Jimmy; it looks like the bleeding is already slowing down. Here." She said, ripping a piece off the bottom of her shirt and handing it to him.

"Put this on it and press hard, you should pull through."

"Uh, excuse me people, but if you're fucking through we're not out of this shit yet." Henry snapped at them while slamming on the breaks.

Sitting in the middle of the street in front of them was an old beat-up station wagon. The doors were all hanging open. What was left of the occupants were scattered all around the area.

There were body parts scattered everywhere, there were enough arms and legs to equal a family of around four or five people.

There were about seven or eight zombies in the immediate area, eating the remains of the corpses. As of yet none of them had noticed the van.

Some of the arms and legs were small, definitely belonging to children.

Henry squeezed his jaw tight, anger flashing in his eyes.

"That's it," he growled "Mary would you please give me a couple of those cocktails we made?" His voice sounded like he was ready to explode at any second.

She reached back and grabbed the first two in the box.

"Are you sure you want to do this Henry" she asked softly while handing the bottles to him.

He looked at her as she sat there waiting for his response, then without saying a word he got out of the van and started to walk over to the car.

"What the fuck's he doing," Jimmy asked Mary.

Her face was dead serious as she looked at Jimmy.

"Getting some payback," she said.

Henry was about ten feet away from the car when he calmly pulled out the lighter he had retrieved from the kitchen drawer of his house. It seemed liked hours ago when in fact only minutes had past. He lit one of the wicks on fire and paused to make sure the cloth had caught the flame. Then with his face set in stone, he threw the bottle at the car.

The bottle hit the side of the station wagon and shattered sending the flaming liquid everywhere within a four foot area. The other bottle landed a second after the first one, landing near the back of the car. The fire spread quick, consuming the car in a blazing fireball. One of the zombies closest to the flames was covered from head to toe with the burning fluid; it was stumbling around with no definite direction.

Then the flaming zombie started walking straight at Henry.

Jimmy was getting ready to jump out of the van to help Henry when he saw Henry take out his handgun and calmly bring it up. When the zombie was no more than two feet away Henry squeezed the trigger, the bullet struck its head right between its eyes.

The back of the skull disintegrated in a fine mist of flaming bone and blood as the now burning corpse fell to the ground like a puppet with its strings cut.

The rest of the zombies had caught fire by now, the homemade napalm burning hot into their cold flesh. Henry turned to walk back to the van. When he was halfway there the gas tank in the old station wagon went up sending the car two feet in the air before the burning wreckage came back down to earth.

As Jimmy and Mary watched, Henry climbed back into the driver's seat, buckled his seatbelt and put the vehicle in drive, then headed down the street at a leisurely pace.

To avoid the burning wreckage he drove onto a beautifully manicured lawn, the van bouncing over the curb to get back onto the street.

"Don't forget to buckle up" he said politely.

Jimmy and Mary just looked at each other.

CHAPTER 21

SCOTT WAS SITTING in the basement, planning his next move. He knew he couldn't stay here long, especially after what had happened to his neighbor.

His time here was quickly running out.

He could hear explosions coming from a few streets over and smell the smoke. Something bad was going down over there. How long before the trouble came this way? Plus more and more of those things were showing up outside every minute. He thought of the police car again. The lights on its roof had been dimming in the couple of hours since it had arrived. If he was going to make a run for it, he needed to decide quickly before the battery died in the car.

He sat for another minute, biting his lip in concentration; then he decided to go for it.

He packed a backpack full of as much water as he could carry without the weight slowing him down too much, then he added some canned food to the pack and got ready to go.

Wait", he said to himself. "I need a weapon."

He looked around the cellar, his eyes stopping on a machete hanging in the corner. He had used it many times on the weeds that grew on the border of his land. It had a good weight and he had just sharpened it a few weeks ago. Taking it of the wall he headed upstairs.

It was quiet in the house. He thought about checking the television and then figured what's the point.

No matter what it said, he still needed to get out of here or wind up like his neighbor outside in the street.

Going to his front door he opened it a crack to see what the street looked like. There were five zombies in the immediate area of the squad car, and three in between him and the car.

From watching the scenes earlier in the day he knew they didn't move that fast, so if he was quick, he should be able to make it to the car, jump in and get the hell out to dodge before they could get him. At least that was the plan.

His heart felt like it was going to explode out of his chest, and now he had to go to the bathroom.

So screw it, he put his backpack down and went into the bathroom to take a piss. Things were bad enough without pissing his pants, after all who knows when he'd get another chance to go?

He resisted the urge to wash his hands when he was finished thinking it would probably kill him. Then he buckled his pants back up and went to the door to try again.

Once he had himself back together he took another peek out the door. Everything was the way he'd left it a few minutes ago. He took a few deep breaths to steel himself for the dash to the car when all of a sudden a van came driving down the street.

The odd thing was it wasn't going very fast, like the driver was taking a Sunday drive, although there was one difference. The van kept swerving to run over as many zombies as it could. As he watched it come up the street he saw a zombie go under the undercarriage, coming out the back end a bloody mess, still twitching as it tried to get back up, even with both its legs broken.

The van pulled up near the squad car, the driver evidently having the same idea as Scott.

When the van stopped a zombie came up to the door from the front of the van, when it was right on top of the vehicle the door flew open hitting the zombie hard. As it lost its balance a tall man, with dark hair and a good build on him, jumped out of the driver's seat. He calmly walked over to where the zombie was just starting to get back up. He pulled a gun out of a holster on his hip and shot the zombie in the face. The things' jaw disappeared in a red mist. Before the body had hit the ground he was searching for another target. Another one came up on his side; he dropped to the ground and kicked its legs out from under it. Then blew its head off with another close range shot, the hollow point bullets taking the back of its head clean off.

Scott saw him yell something back at the van, then two more people jumped out.

A young kid jumped out of the passenger door holding a shovel which he immediately used as one of the zombies got to close. When the shovel connected with the zombie's head Scott could hear the clang of the shovel as it hit skull from where he was across the street.

As the zombie went down the kid straddled it and slammed the point of the shovel through its neck. Then with a twitch of his wrist he sent it tumbling down the street. The head rolled for a couple of seconds until coming to a stop in the gutter. To Scott's surprise he could still see the mouth opening and closing, like it was trying to speak, even though it had no vocal chords.

The last person out of the van was a woman. She looked to be in her twenties and as he watched she was running over to the dead cops and grabbing their weapons while the two men kept the zombies away from her. After retrieving the weapons she then headed to the squad car. As she was struggling to get the shotgun she didn't see there was a zombie coming up behind her and the other two guys were busy fending off their own attackers.

Scott decided he wasn't going to just watch another person die.

He bolted from the door, running across the street with his machete held over his head for a downward swing. The zombie had just grabbed the girl but before it could do anything to her he was by her side, his arm coming down.

The machete went straight into the head above the forehead of the thing. The zombie slumped to the ground. Scott tried to pull the machete out of its head but it was jammed in there to tight thanks to the force of his blow. As he kept trying the older man came up to him "Leave it," he grunted at Scott, "we need to go now, there's more coming."

Scott looked to where the man was looking. Back down the street there had to be at least fifty of them coming up the street, with more coming out of adjoining houses.

The man grabbed Scott by his sleeve and gave him a gentle push to the van.

"If you want a ride come on, I can't tell you when the next bus is coming by."

Scott smiled as he climbed into the van with the other people.

Before he pulled away the tall man pulled a bottle filled with some fluid and a strip of cloth in its neck from in between the seats. He lit it then tossed it out the window at the squad car. When the bottle broke the car was engulfed in flame. Then with a satisfied grin on his face he slammed the van in drive and they took off down the road.

Leaving the walking dead far behind them.

CHAPTER 22

COLONEL GEORGE T. Miller of the United States army leaned closer to the glass of the helicopter he was at presently occupying 1,000 feet in the air.

Below him he could see what was left of Main St., of the town now codenamed "Dead water".

There had been an outbreak of some kind of biological agent. Within hours the town's infrastructure had collapsed and now as Miller looked down on what was once a quaint little town in the Midwest, all he saw was devastation.

More than half the town was aflame. With smaller fires popping up as the wind helped spread the conflagrations.

He could see people still walking around on the street, although they didn't seem to be moving with any kind of purpose. Then off to his right on a roof top he saw someone waving frantically.

Miller Tapped his pilot on the shoulder, pointing to where the woman was, he signaled to go in closer. As the helicopter banked in to get a closer look he saw more people arriving on the roof via the emergency access. These people were heading straight for the woman. About six in total had arrived and were now shuffling up behind her.

As Miller's helicopter got a little close he waved to the pilot to bring the bird down for a closer look.

"Can't sir," the pilot said, shaking his head, "Power lines."

Miller sat watching helpless in his seat as the doomed woman waved frantically for help. Miller tried to point behind her, to have her turn around, but he was too high up for her to see him clearly.

The rotors of the helicopter drowned out the footsteps of the zombies as they dragged their feet on the gravel, each step slowly bringing them closer to her.

A second before the creatures were on her she whipped herself around, sensing someone was behind her.

It was too late. Before she could run they swarmed over her, forcing her to the ground by the weight of there numbers. Inside the helicopter Miller stared astonished at the brutality he was witnessing.

The woman's screams were washed away by the rotor blades. Two of the creatures set there jaws into both sides of her neck. The arterial spray shot straight up into the air, and was then dispersed by the rotor blades into a fine mist, which then tinted the roof red.

Miller watched in fascination as her head was severed from her shoulders as claw like hands ripped muscle and bone. The torso of the woman was little more than a pile of meat and gore as the creatures ripped her stomach and chest open, scooping out the soft organs inside and gorging themselves on the bloody mess.

Miller had seen enough. Looking at the pilot's face, mostly hidden behind his helmet and radio gear, Miller wondered what was going through his mind after witnessing the carnage on display below them.

He didn't ask. Instead he signaled the pilot to take them back up and continue on with the recon of the area. There was still a lot to do.

The brass upstairs for once had been on top of things and had made there decisions quickly.

The borders around the affected areas were to be sealed off; no one in or out.

Once order had been regained the affected areas were to be wiped out. There could be no chances taken that this contagion could spread beyond the town's already infected areas.

Scorched earth policy, Miller ground his jaw together. All those people would be slaughtered.

The soldiers at the barricades were being given orders to shoot on sight, regardless if signs of infection were visible or not.

As the sun was beginning to set, the sky was turning orange, leaving long shadows in the streets below as the town continued to burn.

CHAPTER 23

AS THEY HEADED away from the burning station wagon and onto the two lane blacktop no one spoke. Each one of them lost in their own thoughts.

Henry was thinking about Emily, about the last time he had seen her alive that morning.

If only he had known, he would have said so many things to her that now he would never get the chance to say. He blinked away a stray tear, for now pushing those emotions deep down inside and burying them for now. For now he needed to stay sharp. He looked in the rearview mirror seeing Mary's face reflected back, she too was lost in thought, her body swaying gently to the motions of the van. On his right Jimmy sat with his eyes closed, breathing heavily as he pressed the rag to his head, keeping pressure on his wound.

"Thanks for taking me with you," Scott said to no one in particular.

Mary looked at him. "Thank you for helping me back there," she said, smiling at him. "My name's Mary, that's Jimmy and Henry."

The two men each put up a hand and did a quick wave.

"Hey," they both said at the same time.

After a few moments of silence Henry started slowing down. Pulling the van over to the side of the road he put it in park and jumped out.

"Ok people, let's take a breather and do a little inventory, see what we have and don't have. Jimmy, check out those guns we just got. Mary, see how many cocktails we have left." Henry said.

"What'd you say your name was?" Henry asked looking at Scott.

"Uh, Scott Peters. Is there anything I can do?" He asked Henry.

"Well for starters, what's in the backpack?" Henry asked pointing to the bag on the seat.

"Food and water, I had a machete, but well, you know what happened."

"Yeah, its okay you did good."

"Thanks Henry," Scott smiled back.

Jimmy retrieved the two handguns from the van. The weapons were covered in blood and what looked like bits of shaved steak. Jimmy grabbed a rag from inside the van and started wiping the worst of the gore off the guns.

"So where to now, Henry?" Jimmy asked while making a face as a particularly nasty bit of gristle was refusing to dislodge from between the trigger.

"Well, the town line is about two miles down the road, I say we head that way. If this infection or contamination or whatever is happening here is localized then we should be ok at the next town."

"And if it isn't?" Mary asked from inside the van as she was busy organizing boxes.

"Do you want the long answer or the short answer?" Henry asked.

"Short answer," Mary answered back.

Henry's face grew grim "Then we're fucked," he said simply.

Jimmy looked up. "That's not the answer I wanted to hear Henry, shit we've made it this far, haven't we?"

"I just don't understand why no one's come to help us; surely someone outside the town must know what's going on." Scott said.

"Well if they do they're sure taking there god damn time doing something about it." Jimmy said from the other side of the van.

"Well, listen boys I need to use the ladies room, so I'll be right back." Mary said reaching into the van and grabbing some paper. She then walked away a little bit to have some privacy in the shrubs lining the shoulder of the road.

Henry also took the time they had to take a breather and relax. The two lane highway was open on both sides so he felt reasonably safe that nothing could sneak up on them.

"I say we stay here for a while and catch a breather, agreed?" Henry asked the two men.

They both nodded approval and then Mary walked out of the woods.

"Agreed," she said.

Henry looked at her, had she read his mind?

She smiled at him. "Voices carry out here Henry; I could hear you just fine."

He nodded and then clapped his hands. "Well guys I'm starving, lets see what we have to eat.

Together the four of them relaxed and over a simple meal started to become a family.

CHAPTER 24

PRIVATE JAMES MURPHY of the United States National Guard flicked another cigarette butt into the street. The collection of used filters proclaiming he had been here awhile. The sun had set an hour ago and the spotlights set up around the blockade cast long shadows that reached into the surrounding woods. The highway was quiet, had been since himself and the other three men in his squad had set up camp. He didn't know the full details of what the hell was going down, but his squad had orders to shoot anyone who came up this road on sight. The infection could not be released into the rest of the state or possibly the whole country. That was fine by him. Murphy liked to shoot things, especially if he got to kill them. If murder was legal he would be the happiest man alive.

When James Murphy was a child he loved to torture small animals, he loved to see that spark be extinguished from there eyes as he squeezed their necks until they snapped.

As he grew older he had graduated to larger animals.

One night a few years ago he had even snuck onto one of the farms in the area and killed a horse. First he had sliced its throat, then when the animal had fallen to the ground from blood loss, he reached under its belly and cut from end to end, reveling in the blood as it poured onto his arms and covered his legs. Then he had gutted the creature and left the remains scattered along the hill where the carcass had fallen.

That night he had gone home and masturbated and while still covered in the animal's blood had had one of the most intense orgasms of his life.

Yes, Private James Murphy liked to kill and now the United States government was giving him permission to kill the one animal he had never killed before.

Murphy's face had a smile on from ear to ear just thinking about how it would go down when he saw a station wagon coming up the road. "Perfect," he said.

As the car slowly approached him he put up his hand for the vehicle to slow down. The car decelerated and then came to a stop about twenty feet from where Murphy stood. A man stuck his head out the window and yelled to Murphy.

"Please, we need help, my wife and daughter are sick; I think they caught whatever's in the water. Can you help us?"

Murphy smiled as he walked over to the car. "Buddy, you don't know the half of it." He said as his smile became serious.

When he was only a few feet from the car he unslung his rifle and aimed it at the man in the car. The man just sat there, unable to believe what he was seeing. These men were supposed to help them.

Murphy raised his rifle and fired at the driver, the bullet entering the front windshield at an angle. The bullet was deflected by the windshield just enough for it to miss the man's head. Instead it just blew off his left ear. The man reached up to his ear and felt blood and quicker than Murphy would have thought possible the man slammed the car in reverse and started backing up as fast as the car would go. Murphy started firing at the car while his fellow soldiers fired their rifles from behind him into the car as well.

Murphy was in heaven, he fired wildly at the car, too lost in the moment to really concentrate. A state of euphoria came over him as he sent bullet after bullet at the car.

By a miracle the car was still moving as nothing vital had been damaged, the driver spun the car on its wheels and drove off back the way it had come.

Murphy's shoulder's sagged as he watched the car recede into the distance.

He was so close to a kill. Why did he jump the gun and start shooting so early?

As he walked back to the blockade his buddies asked if he thought he had got any of them. He just shrugged and went back to smoking cigarettes by the pile he had previously made.

Next time he would make sure he got the drop on his victims. He'd make sure they wouldn't see it coming.

An evil smile crossed his lips as he took a drag from his cigarette.

Oh Yes, Private James Murphy was looking forward to tonight.

CHAPTER 25

THOMAS WILLIAMS, TOMMY to his friends, was a zombie.

The last thing the living Thomas Williams remembered was sitting down to lunch at the corner deli on Main St. and having a nice hot cup of homemade chicken soup. Then he had felt dizzy and then . . . . blackness.

Thomas Williams' brain was dead, the body functioning automatically on instinct, an insatiable hunger driving it on. It had been on Main St. when Henry had blown the gas truck.

During the fire it had been burned, and had been separated from its brethren. The fire had blocked its main path so it had wandered into the woods at the end of Main St. looking for easier prey.

It had stumbled around for hours but no prey had been discovered. Its hunger was screaming inside it. Then when the hunger was becoming unbearable it spotted a camping site.

A hiker had set up camp and had decided to catch a nap before moving on and finishing the trail. The man had been isolated out in the forest so had no idea what had been transpiring a few miles away. When the man had heard the sound of the tanker truck exploding he had assumed it was thunder as the sky was overcast and had then stretched out to relax; soon sleeping from his exertions that day.

Shuffling over to the clearing the zombie approached the campsite.

On the ground, curled up in a sleeping bag was a man, his eyes were closed and his chest rose slowly in tune with his breathing. The late Thomas Williams walked up to him and fell to the ground its teeth going for the man's throat in one fluid motion. The man's eyes snapped open. He was able to get off one scream before bloody teeth ripped out his larynx and he started to drown in his own blood. The body spasmed a few more times in its death throes then lay still. Thomas Williams continued to feed until its stomach ruptured inside its abdomen, not stopping until every morsel was consumed.

But the hunger was still there; never could it be extinguished; only quelled temporarily.

So Thomas Williams moved on, searching for more prey.

After the sun had gone down, with the woods as black as coal, Thomas Williams saw what if he could still reason he would have deduced as a spotlight.

With the light like a lighthouse off the New England shore calling ships to port Thomas Williams turned and headed for it.

The hunger was once again screaming inside him to be satisfied.

CHAPTER 26

THE FOURSOME STAYED on the side of the highway until the sun set. The road was quiet, as they had given themselves a little distance from populated areas. They used the time to clean themselves up a bit, and to have dinner consisting of canned goods and bottled water.

Scott added his supplies to the group's food stores giving them a couple of day's worth of supplies. Though Henry was pretty positive their ordeal was over and ten more minutes on the road should get them out of town and to safety.

Mary and Jimmy were at the back of the van talking softly together, while Henry was under the hood of the van checking its fluids and making sure nothing had been seriously damaged in their rush to escape from his house.

Scott was by his side, watching the man work.

"Do you think this plague is everywhere?" He asked Henry.

"Don't know," Henry answered back while checking the oil dipstick, wiping it clean on his pant leg then slipping it back in its tube. "But I'll tell you this, whatever happens I'm not going down without a fight." He punctuated this last sentence by slamming the hood closed.

It didn't fit as tight as it used to due to the abuse it had seen today, but it stayed down, the hood latch still catching.

"What do you say we get out of here?" He yelled to the back of the van.

The couple turned around and came forward to get back in the van.

Jimmy had one of those smiles on his face like when a boy sneaks his first kiss from a girl he likes, as he jumped into the front seat.

Henry smiled to himself, remembering those days with Emily when they had first met.

Images of her dead body lying on their kitchen floor slammed back into his head.

He shook his head to shake them loose, putting them in the back of his mind.

"All right" Henry asked like a diligent parent. "Did everyone go to the bathroom?"

Mary chuckled at this, while Scott just stared, not quite getting it. Jimmy just shook his head. "Just fucking drive old man." He said trying to sound annoyed.

Henry smiled to himself, pulling the van back onto the road.

He even clicked his turn signal on as he changed lanes and headed down the road at a moderate rate of speed

CHAPTER 27

MURPHY LOOKED UP from stepping on yet another cigarette butt to see two tiny lights headed for him. He gauged the lights to be about a half a mile away. They'd be on top of him in a minute or two.

Murphy doubled checked the safety on his rifle, as he raised his weapon and pointed it at the oncoming lights. Licking his lips in anticipation he smiled, this was gonna be good. He wouldn't make the same mistakes twice.

Henry slowed the van to a crawl as he noticed lights around the bend in the road.

"Something's up there." He said.

"Who do you think it is?" Mary asked from the backseat.

"Help?" asked Scott. "The police maybe?"

"I dunno," said Henry," but we'll be there in a minute so get ready."

"Who the fuck else would it be, just go." Jimmy snapped. Thanks to his scalp wound his head was killing him, and he was short on patience.

Henry looked over at Jimmy as he was adjusting the bandage Mary had helped put on him earlier.

Then let his foot off the brake and headed towards the lights.

As they got a little closer they could make out a soldier standing in front of a blockade.

Two camouflaged military trucks were parked in the middle of the road with their bumpers touching. Two spotlights, one each side of the road rained white light down on the area; the shoulder of the road was wreathed in darkness. Henry noticed absently that there probably wasn't enough room to try to blow by the barricade on the sides, not that he thought he would need to.

When they were about two-hundred yards and closing Henry saw the soldier raising his hands for them to stop. He appeared to be non hostile as Henry moved the minivan closer.

Then before anyone in the car could say anything one of the soldiers by the trucks started firing on them, peppering the van with bullets.

"What the fuck is that asshole doing? We're friendly." yelled Jimmy.

The first bullet hit the top of the windshield, cracking it. Henry slammed on the brake.

He could feel other bullets hitting the van as he tried to turn the van around and get the hell out of there.

As the van was sideways in the road he felt the air of a bullet fly through his open window, past his nose and exit out Jimmy's window. In passing Henry realized if Jimmy had been leaning forward the bullet would have hit him right in the left side of his face, killing him instantly.

Then as Henry completed a hasty u-turn and retreated back the way they'd come, he looked in his rearview.

The bullets had stopped and when he saw what was transpiring behind him, he smiled. "Serves you right you bastard," Henry thought.

The break lights of the van got smaller until they disappeared from view

Murphy frowned when his buddies jumped the gun and started firing too soon but quickly overcame his disappointment as he proceeded to fire at the van as well.

Once again he felt the thrill of the kill; this was what he lived for. He fired two rounds before the vehicle had a chance to turn around. The minivan had stopped and was trying to make a hasty u-turn.

Murphy kept firing. He had the driver in his sights and was about to pull the trigger and blow the man's head off when something popped up on his left side out of the woods.

On Murphy's left a shadow started forming out of the blackness created by the spotlights.

Murphy didn't notice as he had tunnel vision only for the van. He heard his buddies yelling something but he couldn't make it out over the noise of his rifle. He didn't realize anything was wrong until he suddenly felt searing pain coming from his left shoulder. He jumped back yelling and turned to stare into the face of death. The man standing before him with a piece of his arm in his mouth did not look healthy. The lips were pulled back showing the whites of the teeth all the way to the gums. Or Murphy assumed they would have been white if they hadn't been stained red with his own blood. One eye had a tree root sticking out of it. The ruptured eyeball was leaking down across its cheek. Murphy gagged from the smell. It reminded him of those days when he had left those animals to rot in the woods and when he had been through with them he had come back days later to bury them. The smell of decomposing meat had permeated the area. This man smelled worse. The man's hair was burned off his head, the skin peeling from his scalp. Murphy took one look and wondered how the hell this man could be walking around?

Murphy got his rifle up as it advanced on him. He fired two shots into its chest and abdomen.

The zombie's stomach already full and ruptured exploded out onto the road. Meat and intestines poured out of it. It didn't slow down; within seconds it was on Murphy, forcing him to the ground.

Its teeth bit into Murphy's cheek, ripping away a two inch chunk of flesh.

By now the other soldiers were next to Murphy, trying to get it off him. Murphy's flailing hands tried to push the zombies face away from his, two of his fingers slipping into the zombie's mouth by accident. The teeth clamped down to the bone, blood squirting into its mouth and dripping out and down back on to Murphy's face, temporarily blinding him.

Then one of the other soldiers took his rifle butt and slammed the zombie in the face. Cartilage gave way to metal as the gun butt flattened the side of its face, knocking teeth to the ground. The second time the gun butt hit its head the impact knocked the zombie off Murphy where another soldier had his rifle raised and fired, blowing the head off from the nose up. The zombie wavered for a moment and then with Murphy's help fell over to the ground. With what was left inside the skull oozing onto the pavement. Murphy's face was a red mess, as he screamed for a medic.

As one of his buddies radioed back to base for help, a bird cried off in the woods.

To an untrained ear it sounded an awful lot like laughter.

CHAPTER 28

THE HIGHWAY WAS quiet, nothing stirred. A lone squirrel crossed the highway searching for food. The road was empty and had been for most of the previous day.

The animal felt safe enough to venture forth onto the blacktop as the foraging had always been better on the other side of the road. When it was halfway across the road it felt a tremor under its paws through the warm tar, as it cooled off in the night air.

It looked up to see two bright lights barreling down on it. It froze, not thinking which way to run, as the giant metal beast bore down on it. The front tire crushed its upper body and as the back tire rolled over it to finish the job it had time for one quick screech. Then its head was crushed flat by the rolling tires, and it knew no more. The road was quiet once more.

Henry felt a slight bump as his wife's minivan hurled down the highway. Only moments had passed since escaping the blockade and as the adrenaline was pumping time seemed to stand still. After a few more minutes of frantic driving Henry could see no signs of pursuit in his rearview mirror and had brought the vehicle to a more manageable speed.

"Jesus Christ!" Jimmy screamed. "Those fucking assholes were trying to kill us. What the fuck for?"

"Christ, I don't know why!" Henry yelled back. "But I know we're not getting out that way!"

"Do you think they could have all the roads out of town blocked like that one, Henry?" Scott asked from the back seat. Everything had happened so fast he had barely had time to take it all in before it was over and the van had been screaming away back down the highway.

"What if we try another direction," he finished.

"But that would mean we would have to backtrack from the way we just came." Mary said next to Scott. "We'd have to fight our way back through those things again to get to the other side."

"Shit Mary, what other options do we have? We can't stay on the highway forever and the towns not safe, even if we had enough food and water, sooner or later those things would get us too."

Jimmy explained this to her. Then turned to Henry, and said, "You know Henry if we go straight through and don't stop we should be able to plow right through any of them that are in the streets."

Henry sighed, as the adrenaline left his system he was feeling tired, the whole day creeping up on him and hitting him all at once. He was tired and as he looked at the faces of his new friends, he could see the same weariness reflected back to him.

In the distance his headlights reflected off an old highway sign, proclaiming food and gas only a 1/2 mile away.

"Well I don't know about you guys but I've had enough for one day, there's a gas station up the road. Let's check it out, if it's safe we'll stay there tonight and then decide what to do in the morning."

"Jimmy, Scott, and Mary all agreed, until Henry had brought it up none of them had realized how weary they were.

Henry continued down the road feeling at least a little better knowing they had a destination.

The gas station appeared on the left side of the road and Henry pulled in, the brakes squeaking a little as he came to a stop, the front tires rolling over a wire in the dirt. There was the sound of a buzzer, it buzzed twice then stopped. They exited the van together and looked around the station. It was dark, with no signs of being occupied.

"Scott, would you see if the pumps work?" Henry asked. "We should top off the gas tank if we can, who knows where else we'll be able to get gas again." Henry said as he jumped out of the minivan.

"Sure Henry," Scott said heading over to the pumps.

"I'll check inside," Jimmy said as he started walking over to the door to the building. His boots kicked up a ball of dust as he walked.

"Mary, why don't you stay her with me until we know the coast is clear?" Henry suggested.

"Sure Henry, fine." She was too exhausted to argue and couldn't wait to finally get some rest.

She headed back to her seat in the van and plopped down exhausted.

Jimmy opened the screen door and entered the small ten by eight sized room; it smelled of old cigarettes and oil. There was another odor behind those smells, one of mold or mildew.

His shoes slipped a little on the floor as he closed the door behind him. He hoped it was oil on the floor as in the dark he couldn't tell. His hand felt along the wall for a light switch.

After a moment or two of fumbling around his hand made contact with something that felt like a light switch, he flicked it up and down a few times. Nothing happened, "Shit," he said under his breath.

The power was off. Through the moonlight filtering in through the dusty side window he could see the place was empty. At the back of the room there was one door. On the front of it in peeling black letters was the word 'restroom'. Jimmy relaxed a little, the place was empty and for the time being they were safe.

"Jimmy!" Henry called from outside. "Is everything ok in there?"

"It's empty," Jimmy called back. "Nothing in here but dirt and some old cigarettes; and the powers off."

"I know," Henry agreed, "Scott thinks he can siphon some gas from some of the cars out back, want to give us a hand?"

"Sure," Jimmy replied, "I'll be right out." Turning to leave he thought he heard scratching. He paused in mid turn; he slowed his breathing, trying to pick out any sounds floating in the air beyond what his friends were doing out front.

Then he heard it again, a soft scratching, like when a dog scratches at the kitchen door to be let outside. It seemed to be coming from behind the bathroom door. He hesitated for a second thinking he should go tell the others, and then he heard it again, accompanied by a soft mewling.

He turned and walked over to the door, hand reaching out to open it, his hand tightened around the knob and turned. With the latch on the door unlocked the door exploded outward, sending Jimmy flying back across the room. Immediately he was smothered by something big, he could feel its breath on his neck, his hands were trapped between himself and its body, he couldn't move. He closed his eyes and waited for its teeth to sink into his throat, ripping it out to feed on his flesh.

Then he felt a wet tongue on his face. Licking him? With the light a little brighter at the front of the room Jimmy was now able to make out what had landed on him. It was a dog. The animal kept licking his face, happy to see someone and be let out of its tiny prison.

When Jimmy felt that his heart didn't feel like it was going to explode out of his chest anymore he got back to his feet, and feeling a little silly, headed back outside with a new friend in tow.

CHAPTER 29

HENRY WAS ABOUT to go get Jimmy when he saw him come walking out of the gas station's door, followed by a black Labrador retriever.

"Well, well what have we got here?" Henry said getting down to one knee so the dog could lick his face.

"I found him in the bathroom," Jimmy said," He pretty much scared the shit out of me."

Mary had also come over to pet the dog." Well at least someone else made it." She said while scratching the dog's ears.

Jimmy looked around." Where's Scott?" he asked.

"He's out behind the station, trying to siphon some gas from some of the old cars back there. Actually someone should go check on him. Henry replied while looking to the back of the gas station.

"I'll go," Mary said as she looked down at the dog. "C'mon boy, come and keep me company."

As she headed out back Jimmy smiled at Henry," Looks like Mary found a friend."

"Yeah, maybe," was all Henry said as Mary and the dog went around the end of the gas station and were lost from sight.

Scott spit gas out of his mouth, the taste overwhelming him for a second. Siphoning gas from two cars so far, he had accumulated about three gallons. The five gallon fuel tank he found was almost filled and then he'd be finished. He spit again, wishing he had some water to wash his mouth out with. The darkness was almost total where he was, the roof of the gas station blocking the moonlight. The siphon hose had run dry again, taking it out he headed for the next car.

He paused for a moment, looking into its window. Was there someone in it?

The shadows had played tricks on his eyes before since he had come back here.

He slowly crept closer, careful not to make a sound with his feet.

When his left foot accidentally kicked a bottle, he thought he was going to jump right out of his shoes. When he was right on top of the car, the clouds shifted a little allowing more moonlight to filter down. The shadows dispersed around the car showing Scott the ripped headliner of the car had sagged down to the dashboard fooling him once again.

He chuckled to himself and walked over to the side of the car.

And walked right into a zombie, the thing reached out for him, grabbing his shirt, buttons ripped as he tried to pull away. The thing followed him step for step. "Help!" he yelled, still trying to pull away.

He tried punching it in the chest but it had no effect.

As the two of them backed into the clearing between the cars and the gas station the moonlight showed Scott clearly who his attacker was.

The thing wore a pair of dirty coveralls, its face covered in grease, the eyes were sunk into its head, staring blankly at nothing, yet still seeing.

"Clyde" was stitched in red embroidery on the breast pocket of what was once the gas station owner.

Clyde had owned and ran the gas station for twenty years and had thought he would have run it for twenty more. At least that was the plan until he had a cool glass of ice water this morning and had died minutes later. His body had sat in the sun all day, cooking in the heat. He hadn't moved at all since he had come back from the dead, just sat there waiting; waiting for someone like Scott to show up.

The zombie reached out again to pull Scott to him, Scott flailed, as he tried to push it away, but the thing's grip was to strong. As the zombies head went in to bite Scott's neck, its head exploded, brains and blood covering Scotts' face, bits of shattered bone stinging him, some leaving shallow scratches on his cheek and forehead.

What was once Clyde fell to the earth like a sack of potatoes, landing with a dull thump. Scott just stood there too astonished to move, then he heard the sound of footsteps and Henry, Mary, and Jimmy ran up to him.

Henry's Glock was in his hands, a thin wisp of smoke still coming from the end.

"Thanks, Henry," Scott wheezed. "Jesus Christ thanks a lot."

Henry just grinned, "Don't thank me to much; I was aiming for its shoulder."

Henry looked at Jimmy, "Get the gas can would you, I think its time we move on."

"Amen" Jimmy replied back. The dog was sniffing around its former master, licking some of the blood from its coveralls. "Oh gross, c'mon boy we'll get something real for you to eat." Mary said while pulling the dog away and leading him back to the van.

While Jimmy filled the vans' gas tank, Mary fed the dog and Henry stood watch, nothing else was going to catch them off guard. Scott used some water sparingly from their meager stores to wash the blood and brains from his face, and flush out the small scratches he had received. Luckily they hadn't broken the skin. Then he went to talk with Henry.

"What did you mean back there when you said you were aiming for that thing's shoulder?" Scott asked while trying to fix his ripped shirt—without much luck—all the buttons were gone.

"Well, I'm not that good a shot, I figured I'd hit it in the shoulder, and slow it down until we could get to you and help. Guess I just got lucky."

"You got lucky?" Scott asked puzzled.

"Look Scott you're still alive, that should be good enough."

"I guess," Scott decided to change the subject. "So what's next, chief?"

Henry turned to look at Scott who was standing there waiting for an answer, and then glanced at Jimmy and Mary who had walked up beside him as well.

The three of them stood there like three children who were looking to their parents for advice; their faces patiently waiting for an answer.

Without realizing it he had become their defacto leader. He just hoped he was up to it.

CHAPTER 30

HENRY TURNED AWAY from Scott and walked back to the van.

"All right guys, I know I said we should get out of here, but maybe we should stay, at least until the sun comes out. The place should be empty now and there shouldn't be anyone else around for miles, I say we post watches and sleep in the van. I know I'm pretty god dam tired of running around this fucking town. This has been one hell of a day," He looked at the others." Well, Opinions?"

"Sounds fine to me Henry," Jimmy answered back. "So, who stands first watch?"

"I will," Scott said quickly. "After what just happened I'm still pretty pumped up. I'll take the first watch."

"Sounds good to me," Henry said back. "Here take this." Henry said, handing him his Glock. "Keep it, I'll use the shotgun. You should be armed anyway. Just point and shoot, the safety's off."

Scott nodded and walked away to stand near the back of the gas station.

"One of us will relieve you in two hours." Henry called over to Scott.

"Kay," Scott said back as he turned to walk around a little and check the other side of the building.

After Henry had worked out who would stand watch, everyone agreed to get some rest.

Henry sat in the driver's seat with Jimmy next to him in the front of the van, and Mary curled up on the backseat with her new best friend on the floor of the van.

Within minutes everyone was fast asleep.

Henry slowly came awake as Scott continued to shake him. Scott's voice becoming clearer as the fog of sleep receded from his mind.

"Henry," Scott whispered, wake up dammit, we've got problems. Something's coming down the highway, I can see headlights."

With that Henry woke up, the fuzziness of sleep washed away by adrenaline.

"Who's coming down the highway, how many?"

"Don't know but I don't think we should be out in the open when they show up."

"Good idea. Wake the others up, I'm gonna go take a look," Henry said while stepping out of the van.

As Henry walked away, he could hear Scott rousing the others behind him. He ran to the end of the driveway and looked up the highway. Sure enough there were two sets of headlights heading there way.

Henry ran back to the others who were now awake and had just been informed of the situation from Scott.

"What do we do?" Jimmy asked Henry, while he wiped sleep from his eyes. Only about an hour had passed since they had fallen asleep.

"Jimmy, pull the van around back and park it with the other cars back there, with the beating it's taken lately it should blend right in. The rest of us should go hide in the woods until we can see whose coming. Maybe we'll get lucky and they won't stop here."

"Got it, "Jimmy said while hopping into the van and driving it to the back of the station. The rest of them headed over to the edge of the parking lot where the woods were slowly growing back onto the lot, the edges of blacktop splitting as tree roots pushed up through the cement. Jimmy soon joined them moments before the headlights were upon them. They all hunkered down and waited, some holding there breathe with anticipation.

Moments later two jeeps pulled into the gas station lot. Two men were in each of the jeeps. From the uniforms they were wearing they were obviously soldiers, either Army or National Guard. The four of them jumped out of the jeeps hooting and hollering like they were out partying on a Saturday night instead of on patrol. One of the soldiers started walking towards the groups' hiding place, almost like he knew they were there.

Henry raised his gun but stayed motionless; hoping the rest of them did the same.

The dog growled low in his throat and Mary quickly shushed him quiet. Luckily due to the noise the soldier's buddies were making, the soldier approaching them didn't hear anything unusual.

Then when Henry thought he was going to walk right into them he stopped, unzipped his zipper, and then urinated onto the blacktop, the urine steaming in the cool night air. When his business was finished he zipped up and headed back to his buddies. The soldiers were so loud they had attracted a zombie who had been wandering around the woods, the soldiers yelling and swearing at one another was enough for it to pinpoint their location like a beacon. The zombie cleared the woods and walked onto the gas station driveway. From a cursory glance you wouldn't be able to tell it was a zombie, not with the shadows from the trees blocking the moonlight on its face. It was still relatively cleanly dressed, with its shirt still tucked into its pants and the face not showing too much deterioration.

When the soldiers took notice of the man walking towards them they didn't even hesitate. They brought their rifles up and riddled the corpse with bullets. Arms and legs were blown off by the barrage of bullets. The head disappeared in a mist of brains and bone matter.

The zombie dropped to the ground, whatever it was that was keeping it animated extinguished before it hit the ground.

Laughing the soldiers walked over to admire their kill.

"You think it was one of them?" asked one of the soldiers to the others.

"Who cares, are orders are to shoot anything that moves," another answered.

"Come on we better get going if we're late the Colonel will kill us."

With grunts and murmurs of agreement the soldiers went back to their jeeps and drove off down the highway. There break lights quickly disappearing from view.

Henry and the others crept out of their hiding place. They were playing a whole new game now. They had zombies that wanted to eat them and soldiers that wanted to shoot them and they were trapped in the middle.

Henry shrugged; he couldn't do anything about it tonight. Rounding up the others they all went back to the van to get some sleep.

It took a little longer for sleep to come after the spectacle they had witnessed but sooner or later exhaustion won out and they were all soon fast asleep again; as the weight of the day sent them into a dreamless slumber.

Henry groaned as he tried to roll over in his seat, he stopped when he realized he couldn't.

The sun was coming up over the trees and the sky was clear. He looked over to see Scott fast asleep next to him.

He turned his head to see Mary asleep again on the seat after standing her watch last night. They had each stood watch for about two hours.

Jimmy had finished with the last watch and so had got to sleep the longest. When Jimmy saw Henry stirring in the van he walked over to the driver's side window.

"Good Morning, Henry, how was your night?" Jimmy asked with a smile. "Fucking terrible, my neck is killing me. Do me a favor, the next time we have an apocalypse make sure we grab some sleeping bags?"

Jimmy's smile got a little wider "Sure Henry, no problem, I'll make a note of it." "I'm glad the sun's up, it was fucking creepy out here alone in the dark," Jimmy continued. "Should we wake the others up?"

"Nah," Henry shook his head. "Let them sleep, its not like we're on a schedule." After the soldiers had departed the group had went back to sleep, the rest of the night thankfully being uneventful.

While rubbing his neck he got out of the van to stretch. It was a new day and they were still alive, he felt heartened by that fact. He walked over to the end of the driveway to relieve himself. As the pressure on his bladder lessened he felt better.

By the time he returned the others were going about the routines of waking up. "Hey Jimmy," Henry said "before we leave go back into the gas station and grab anything we might be able to use." As an afterthought he added "Please," Jimmy nodded agreeably.

Jimmy walked back over to the station's screen door, as he entered, it didn't seem so bad in the daylight. He looked down onto the floor to see it stained with oil." One mystery solved." He said to himself, thinking back to last night. On a closer examination he found a few things that might come in handy, he packed them up into an old cigarette box and carted them back to the van.

Arriving at the van he saw that everyone was getting ready to go, everyone was anxious to get moving, despite where they were headed. Driving back through Henry's neighborhood was the only way to get to the city limits on the other side of town and hopefully avoid the army if they had patrols about. They had no way of knowing where they might be or what to expect. Jimmy handed the box to Henry who ruffled through it quickly. A few things caught his eye, a pair of binoculars which he put on the van's dashboard, as well as an extra cigarette lighter. The other things such as paper towels and pens he left in the box, to be stowed in the van. As an afterthought he reached back in the box and retrieved a pen, clicked it once to make sure it worked, then put it in his back pants pocket. All his life he had always carried a pen. Old habits die hard, as his father used to tell him.

"All right, we ready to go?" Henry asked the air. As no one objected he jumped into the van, started the engine, and headed out of the parking lot.

It was a little more crowded in the van as they now had an extra passenger, the lab sitting on the seat with its head on Mary's lap.

As he headed onto the road he couldn't have seen the nail the back tire rolled over, puncturing the tire but for now, not leaking.

The van continued down the highway as the sun continued to rise in the sky.

CHAPTER 31

THE VAN SLOWLY drove down the highway, the brakes squeaking softly every time Henry pressed the pedal. The rhythm of the van was soothing and Mary felt herself dozing off. Almost immediately she started dreaming, her unconscious mind trying to put together everything she had been witness to in the past day.

In her dream she was going to visit her parents, she hadn't seen them in a while and was driving down to visit them on her weekend off. The sky was a clear blue as she drove down the interstate. The 80's station was on the radio, a song from her childhood came on, making her think back to when she was young and the weight of the world hadn't started pressing down on her quite so much yet. Singing to the song she noticed her exit coming up, changing lanes she drove down the off ramp. Taking a few rights and lefts she soon found herself turning onto her parent's street.

Everything was just how it should be. All the lawns were carefully manicured as the houses all had new paint or vinyl siding. The road was clean of trash. No cigarette butts or soda cans in these gutters. People she had known since she was a little child waved from their porches or while they were walking their dogs. At the end of the street she turned into the driveway of the only place she would ever really call home. Getting out of the car she wondered why her parents weren't outside to greet her. The thought passed with a flutter as she grabbed her overnight bag from the trunk of her car and headed up the walkway to the front door.

Reaching for the doorknob, she turned it, the door opening quietly on greased hinges.

The gloom was all pervasive as she entered the foyer, the sun peeking in around the curtains.

She walked into the living room, calling out for her parents. No answer came.

Then from the kitchen she heard noises, almost like growls really; and ripping sounds, like when a watermelon is only cut half way and you have to spread it open with your hands.

"Mom, Dad? It's Mary I'm here," she said while walking closer to the kitchen.

Walking into the kitchen she was stopped cold by the sight in front of her.

Her parents were sitting at the table and her new black Labrador retriever was spread out on the kitchen table with its stomach ripped open, blood was everywhere. The dog's intestines were hanging over its carcass, some slipping onto the floor. Before she could do or say anything her parents stood up and started walking towards her.

"Fresh meat," her dad said. A red smile creased his face. And then their clawed hands were reaching out to grab her and drag her down to hell.

Mary awoke with a start, checking her watch she saw only about twenty-five minutes or so had past since they had left the gas station. To say that traffic was light was an understatement, more like nonexistent. There had been a few abandoned cars on the highway, the occupants gone, nothing remarkable about them other than the fact that they had been abandoned.

Then the van had come upon one vehicle that was definitely more noticeable than the others.

The station wagon was riddled with bullet holes and one tire was flat.

The inside was painted in blood, the windows so covered you couldn't see inside. Flies were everywhere, feeding on the blood. As to what may have been inside the car, well, none of them cared to stop and look. After all what would be the point?

As the van slowly rolled around the car Jimmy stared at the windows, his curiosity getting the better of him. When the van was even with the other car's windows Jimmy grabbed Henry's arm. "Henry wait, stop the van." He said peering more closely at the windows. "I think someone's inside that car."

Henry sneered not even looking in Jimmy's direction.

"That's crazy," he said, "It must be 100 degrees in that car, and with all the windows rolled up, no way."

Jimmy continued to stare though. Then without warning something hit the wagon's window so hard it shook it on its frame.

"Ahh," Jimmy yelled, jumping back in his seat. "What the fuck was that?"

Henry stopped the van and backed up a little, returning to the side of the car and putting the van in park. He reached between the seats to retrieve the shotgun and started to open his van door.

"Wait," Jimmy called, "where the hell are you going? We don't know what's in there."

"We will in a second. You two stay here, I'll be right back," Henry said looking at Scott and Mary. The two agreed, with Scott throwing up his hands in surrender and issuing a "No problem, Henry, knock yourself out."

Henry stepped around to the front of the van, scanning the area for any sign of movement.

All was quiet. Except in the car where something was very definitely moving now.

Henry walked over to the car, cocking the shotgun as he moved closer and got a good look at what was once a human being. Man or women was anybody's guess. The hair was almost nonexistent, and the face was nothing but muscle and tendons, the skin having rotted off.

Due to the body being trapped in the car for more than twenty-four hours, with the temperature inside probably exceeding one-hundred degrees, the body had decomposed more rapidly, causing it to become a heaping pile of meat and bones. Perhaps whatever plague was causing this was also speeding up the decomposition of the bodies, either way the thing inside the car was nasty.

As Henry got a little closer he could now smell the odor emanating off the car.

Thank God the windows were rolled up, he thought, or the smell would've been unbearable.

The banging on the window continued, getting louder with each passing second. Then the window exploded outward, some of the shards peppering Henry as he shielded his face with his arms. When the onslaught was finished, Henry looked around his arms to see a writhing zombie crawling out the window and landing in a heap on the hot tar of the highway. Was it Henry's imagination or did the zombies exposed appendages seem to sizzle on the ground like bacon on a grill. The odor was overwhelming; Henry could feel the bile rising in his throat as he fought to keep it down by breathing through his mouth.

Jimmy had opened his door and was about to jump out and help him when he had to jump back to keep out of the zombies reach.

"Don't Jimmy, stay in the van, I got this," Henry said through gritted teeth.

The zombie had started crawling towards Henry now, leaving a slimy red trail behind it.

The black Labrador started barking in the car wanting to get out and attack the rotting animated corpse.

As the zombie reached up on its knees to grab Henry, he brought the shotgun level with its throat and fired one shell point blank. The shell entered the zombie where the chest and throat met, ripping it to threads and shattering its spine on the way out its back, leaving a gaping hole. With its spine severed the zombies head fell limp against its chest. Despite the catastrophic damage it still moved, Henry calmly put the shotgun to its temple and squeezed the trigger, the head disintegrated, blowing brains over the hot tarmac.

"Stay down you bastard." Henry said with hate in his eyes. Then turned and walked back to the van.

After getting back inside he turned to face Jimmy and just sat there looking at him.

"What," Jimmy said while putting his hands into the air? "What I do?"

"Do me a favor, Jimmy will yah, the next time you see something, keep it to yourself."

"Ahh, Ok?" Jimmy said perplexed.

Then Henry smiled at him and the mood lightened as he shifted into drive and continued down the highway, leaving the station wagon behind.

Inside the station wagon another rotting zombie crawled out the open door, finally free of its prison. When the little girl and her mother had "turned" there had been no one to eat but the father, both mother and daughter had overwhelmed him and ripped him to pieces. Then they had been alone in the locked car, not having enough intelligence to open the doors.

Now the girl's mother was spread out on the pavement, as she climbed out into the sun she turned and headed off into the woods. Some dormant memory from her previous life surfacing, telling her she liked to hike in the woods.

As she headed off into the woods her mouth seemed to smile. Or was it just escaping decomposing gas?

It didn't really matter as there was no one to witness it but the trees.

CHAPTER 32

THE VAN ROLLED onto the first street of Henry's neighborhood and slowly came to a halt. The street looked quiet, a little to quiet.

"Where'd they all go?" Jimmy asked while looking up the street.

"They probably went back into the houses, when I saw a couple of cops get attacked yesterday, most of those things came out of their houses; they must have gone back inside." Scott replied from the back seat.

"That's good for us," Henry said. "That means there won't be too many of them on the streets and we should be able to just drive through to the other side."

"Well fuck Henry; let's go, the sooner we're through the better." Jimmy said with a touch of nervousness to his voice.

Henry put the van in gear and they started rolling through the streets. A feeling of gloom seemed to suffuse the people in the van. Watching out the windows at all the death and destruction was shocking even after everything they'd been through. What was left of human beings could be seen scattered across the streets, on lawns, hanging out windows and in cars as people not affected by the plague had tried to escape only to be run down and killed by their loved ones.

Numerous houses were on fire, the smoke billowing into the air to be swept away by the wind.

But no zombies could be seen. The van was making pretty good progress weaving its way through the stalled cars in the streets until they started to hear the sound of a helicopter overhead.

Mary looked up, out the van's window and spotted the helicopter as it flew overhead.

"Do you think they're finally coming to help us?" Mary asked, still watching the machine fly overhead.

"I sure hope so," Henry said, "but after they shot at us yesterday I'm not taking anything for granted."

"Amen" Jimmy murmured next to him.

Unfortunately for them the noise of the helicopter was attracting the zombies outside, as they continued down the streets the zombies began to emerge from the shadows where they had been hiding. Henry could already tell he wasn't going to get through without a fight.

"All right kids, it's getting messy out here, be ready for whatever the hell happens." Henry said quickly, while turning the wheel sharply to avoid a group who were coming down the middle of the street directly at the van. By avoiding one group Henry inadvertently ended up heading for some others, he braced himself and hit the gas, punching through them, sending bodies flying around the van. The bangs and the thumps inside the van was deafening as the bodies of the zombies bounced off the hood and front fender. One zombie was hit so bad its body cracked the windshield with the force of its weight.

Henry continued to zig and zag around the zombies until they came upon a group of about twenty. They were scattered in a way that between the zombies and the cars lying in the road there was no way to get through; as the bodies would end up bogging the van down when Henry had to slow down to avoid other cars on the road.

"Mary, get me one of those cocktails ready," Henry barked.

"Jimmy, how's your throwing arm?"

Jimmy's eyes lit up with understanding when he saw Henry looking ahead at the clustered group of zombies headed their way. "I can reach, no problem."

Mary had the cocktail in her hands and handed it to Henry." Good luck," she said.

"Yeah," Henry answered back: "For all of us."

"You ready Jimmy?" Henry asked.

"Yeah man, just light the fucker." Jimmy said as the adrenaline started to flow through his body.

Henry hit the brakes hard, they only had seconds before the van would be surrounded, he lit the fuse and passed it to Jimmy who was already climbing out the window to put his butt on the window frame, his left hand grabbing onto the roof rack for support.

With the cocktail in his right hand, he leaned back and let the bottle fly, then popped back inside.

It landed true to its target, smashing on the ground and sending flaming liquid all over the pants and some torsos of the zombies. Immediately the group of zombies separated as their bodies were consumed by the fire, some of them falling to the ground and twitching before finally remaining still.

The smell of burned meet permeated the air as the bodies burned

A cheer went up in the van as a path opened up for them. Henry hit the gas pedal, hurling them through the gap. The van avoided a few stragglers and then drove on. The tires crushing burned arms and legs as they drove past the small inferno.

There was a concerted sigh of relief when the van drove past the last house.

As they left the housing development behind them all four of them breathed a sigh of relief. Hoping their odyssey in hell was finally over.

Colonel Miller looked down on the neighborhood below him. He had spotted a lone vehicle making its way through the area. He had seen the van avoiding the walkers and had seen them firebomb the streets. After that the helicopter had moved on and the vehicle had been lost from sight. Whoever they were he wished them well, although the fact that they were in the kill zone didn't give them much of a chance. To be in the affected areas was a death warrant.

No one could be allowed to escape; total containment. Those were his orders, and by God he'd carry them out. The fate of millions rested in his hands and the hands of his soldiers.

And he would not fail them. All these things went through his mind as the helicopter banked east to survey another section. The rotors helping the wind spread the smoke into the sky that was drifting up from the burning houses below.

CHAPTER 33

"SHIT," HENRY WHISPERED out of the side of his mouth, this way's blocked too. He took the binoculars away from his face and handed them back to Jimmy, who took another look.

"Think we could get around them?" he asked.

"Nah, the shoulders too soft, we'd be cut to pieces when the van tried to force its way through the mud. Jimmy my boy, we are so fucked." Henry said, shaking his head wearily.

"Come on, lets get back to the others and fill them in, they're all probably wondering where we are."

With that the two men backed out of the outcropping of foliage they had hidden in and proceeded to head back down the highway, while keeping to the shoulder, to prevent them from being seen by the blockade.

A few minutes later, the two men arrived back at the van, immediately grabbing a bottle of water, each of them quickly chugged it down.

"Well?" Mary asked. "What does it look like down there?"

"The road's blocked that way too. I saw at least three soldiers with guns walking around. We're not getting through that way." Jimmy said through a break in finishing his water.

"Shit." Scott said with frustration in his voice. "I don't believe this shit. So where the hell do we go from here?"

"We need to find a place to lay low, maybe wait this thing out," Henry suggested.

For a few moments everyone was silent, trying to think of something.

"After another few seconds of silence, Henry spoke up, "All right, listen, we'll find some where, but first we need to get moving. If those soldiers send out patrols we'll be sitting ducks."

And with that he walked back to the van. With the others following his lead they were soon all in the van and heading down the highway.

They had only been moving for a few minutes when Henry felt something wrong with the van's steering. A constant thump thump was coming from the back of the van.

Henry pulled the van over to take a look at the outside of the vehicle.

"Shit, shit, shit," he yelled." A goddamn flat."

"So, what's the problem?" Scott asked. "Can't we just put the spare on?"

"We could," Henry answered back. "If I had one, Emily got a flat last week and I never got around to getting it fixed."

"I guess we're walking from here on out." Jimmy added.

Mary was looking around the area, with a look of concentration on her face.

"Hey, Jimmy," she called. "Come here a minute."

As he walked up beside her, she pointed into the woods. "Look up there."

Jimmy looked where she was pointing, recognition appearing on his face.

By now Henry and Scott had moved next to them and they were all looking out into the woods. "What the hell are you two doing?" Henry asked, looking out into the woods but not seeing anything remarkable.

"See those two trees that look like a V?" Mary said to Henry while pointing at the spot where Henry should focus his gaze.

"Ok yeah I see it, what about it?" He said with a squint to his eyes as he looked off into the tree line.

"Well look a little to the left. Do you see that antenna sticking up between those branches?"

Henry concentrated a little more, "Nope I don't see shit."

"There," Jimmy said as well, pointing in the same direction, like that would help the situation.

Then like a camera lens coming into focus the antenna became visible to him.

"Wait, yeah I got it, I see it. So what's it for?"

"That," Mary said with a smile. "Is where we're going."

CHAPTER 34

THE AFTERNOON SUN was hot on their heads. They had been walking for a little more than an hour and had decided to take a quick break. Everyone dropped down wherever an inviting patch of ground looked good.

"I'm too old for this shit." Henry gasped, while cracking open a water bottle and drinking deeply.

"Don't have a heart attack on us, Henry." Jimmy laughed at his side.

Henry screwed the cap back on the bottle before passing it to Jimmy.

"I'm not dead yet," he said, wiping his mouth with his sleeve.

Henry looked over at Mary, who was giving the black lab some water by cupping her hands together into a bowl. "How much longer you think before we get there?" he asked her.

She shrugged, her eyes not leaving the black lab. "Another hour or so give or take."

"You really think we'll be safe there?" Scott's said from where he sat behind her on the log they had picked to sit on.

"Well the place is pretty big," Jimmy responded, "and there was only a few people there when Dr. Martin went crazy, so we should be able to take care of anyone who's there."

"How many is a few Jimmy?" Henry asked with a concerned look on his face.

"Well most of the lab techs leave after lunch, and I know some of the experiments were on hold due to funding problems, so there was probably just a skeleton crew on when I took off."

"How many is that in people, Jimmy?" Henry asked, staring back with a hint of impatience in his voice.

"Oh, I'd say about twenty or so."

"Twenty!" Scott squeaked. "You want us to go in that building and kill twenty of those things."

"You know Scott we really don't have much choice." Henry said, spelling it out to the man.

"Number one, we don't have a vehicle, number two, we're low on water, number three, we're trapped in a town with no escape route and bloodthirsty zombies all around us, number four, we need shelter, number five . . . ."

Scott put up his hands in surrender, cutting Henry off. "Ok, ok I get it, we're fucked."

Henry looked at the three people surrounding him, in just a short time he already felt more for these people than some of his relatives that he'd known his whole life.

Picking up his shotgun and leaning it against his shoulder, he smiled.

"Well, maybe a little bit, but where there's life there's hope, and I'll tell you this, I'm hoping to kick some zombie ass.

With that said he turned around and started walking up the hill. Not waiting to see if he was being followed.

The others collected there backpacks and followed him.

To their salvation or their deaths, only time would tell.

The halls of Pineridge labs were dark. The smell of death permeated the walls.

He had killed the last live human hours ago and already his hunger was back.

He needed fresh meat but his now limited intelligence didn't quite comprehend how he could accomplish this task.

Dr. Martin screamed in frustration as he roamed the silent halls.

As the hunger inside him screamed to be fulfilled.

CHAPTER 35

THEY HAD BEEN walking for about an hour when Henry called another break. Everyone dropped down into the soft leaves with a sigh of relief.

"Jesus Christ my feet are killing me. I wonder if your feet hurt when you're a zombie. I mean all those guys do is walk around all day trying to eat us."

"Do you really want to find out Jimmy?" Scott laughed, sitting next to him on the cool ground.

"No, of course not, I was just, you know, making conversation."

"Some conversation Jimmy, that's a horrible thing to say." Mary said in an unapproved tone.

"Sorry Mary, I was just joking around." Jimmy said quietly.

Mary smiled at him. "That's okay. I'm sorry too, I'm just tired."

"We all are," Henry said. "It'll be good to stay in one place for awhile."

"Hopefully," Scott said, as he stretched out on the ground and put his hands behind his head.

It was peaceful where they were. The glade Henry had chosen to take a break in was a natural clearing with fallen logs in the middle and surrounded on all sides by a thin layer of waist high brush. It was a good place to stay and recoup their strength before moving on with the final leg of their journey.

"Well if you boys will excuse me I need to use the ladies room." She said while rummaging in her backpack for some paper towels.

"Why don't you just go over there?" Jimmy asked while pointing at a clump of small trees.

"No thank you Jimmy. You know, we all can't just whip it out and go in any direction we want to. Some of us have a little more restriction in that department.

With that said she walked out of the clearing a ways to find a spot to do her business.

Both Henry and Scott looked disapprovingly at Jimmy after Mary had left the clearing.

"What I do now?" Jimmy said innocently with his hands in the air.

"Jimmy my boy, Henry said to him while shaking his head back and forth. "If you have to ask then it just doesn't matter."

Mary walked a little ways from the men to find a good spot to go to the bathroom.

Not, she thought, that there really was a good spot out in the middle of the woods.

Finding a pretty good spot not to far from the clearing—she could still hear the boys mumbling to each other—she pulled down her pants to go pee.

Because of the awkward position she was squatting in her bladder was being restricted and it was taking longer than she wanted it too.

As she sat there squatting in the middle of the woods she was able to take in how grand the forest really was. It was alive with the sounds of life. Birds were in the trees chirping and over to her right it looked like a family of squirrels was playing. She smiled as she watched them run up and down the trees, like they were playing a game of tag.

She was so preoccupied she didn't realize a small zombie was slowly creeping up on her from behind.

As she finally finished peeing she stood up to readjust her pants and shirt when she heard a twig snap behind her. She turned around to see what looked like a dead eight year old girl coming right at her. The dress it was wearing the only proof that the child was once female.

It was hard to tell as the girl's face was a red mess of torn skin. Her lips were pulled back away from her teeth, leaving the gums exposed in a sick parody of a smile. Her clothes were soaked through with blood and maggots could be seen squirming out of the seams of her dress. The skin on her arms and legs was pulled tight against the muscle and bone of her appendages; making her look like she had starved to death. Her swollen belly completed this picture as Mary stared at the small creature approaching her.

Though Mary was startled she started to back away from the girl until her foot fell into a small hole that had been made by an animal at one time.

Her foot twisted out from under her and she fell to the leaf strewn ground with a scream. Her eyes lost contact with the small zombie for just a moment.

That's when the zombie girl jumped onto Mary.

If Mary had been able to stay upright she probably would have been able to keep the girl at bay easily, but with her butt on the ground she was now at equal heights with the girl. And the girl was taking full advantage of it.

The small zombie jumped onto Mary's chest and tried to bite at her neck.

Mary was able to get her hand under the girl's chin and keep her away. She gagged when her hand sank into the girl's rotted flesh as the girl kept squirming in her grip. The smell was absolutely horrid; Mary could feel the bile rising in her throat. The zombies head was now directly above Mary and as she watched, a maggot wiggled out of the girl's nose and fell off to land in Mary's open mouth. That was it for Mary, her stomach erupted like a volcano, shooting out of her mouth and hitting the zombie in the face. For a second the zombie was blinded by the vomit and its attack lessened a bit. That was enough for Mary to buck her hips and throw the zombie off of her.

She could hear the sounds of footfalls now running through the forest and in a moment the three men were upon her.

The black lab ran up and stood by her side growling protectively at the zombie.

"Holy shit," Jimmy said. "Will you look at that?"

"Wow," Scott said as he stared at the desiccated remains of the little girl who was regaining her feet. "That is really gross."

"Gross!" Mary yelled at them while wiping the vomit of her self. "Try having that fucking thing on top of you. Then tell me what's gross."

The three men new how serious she was if she was cursing, that was the first time they had heard her swear.

The girl was unaffected by any of these exchanges and had started to approach the group, not really knowing who it should attack first.

"Well, what are we going to do with it?" Jimmy asked as he watched the girl approach him. The last thing he'd be is scared, the zombie only being about four feet tall.

"What we do with all of them, we kill it. It sucks that it's a kid but we have to take it out." Henry said, not at all pleased with the decision but knowing it had to be done. He was then surprised when Mary came up next to him and held out her hand.

"I'll do it," she said with vengeance in her eyes.

Henry handed her the shotgun. The look in her eyes brooking no argument.

"It's already cocked, just point and shoot." He said while handing it over to her.

She took it and nodded. Then she calmly walked over to the girl and without preamble shot it in the face.

The tiny face disintegrated; the force of the shot blowing chunks of skull all over the immediate area behind the girl. The small body flew back and struck a tree and then fell on its side as blood ran out of its neck and into the soil.

She then walked back to Henry and handed the weapon back.

"Thank you," she said quietly. Then she went over and stood next to Jimmy.

There was an awkward moment of silence as they all stood there staring at the corpse of the little girl.

Then Jimmy broke the silence as he looked at Mary and asked.

"So Mary, did you get to go to the bathroom?"

Mary's jaw dropped as she turned to look at him, astonished at his audacity.

And then her face blossomed into a smile as she playfully punched him in the arm.

Then she turned around and walked back to the clearing; the dog following at her heels.

Both Henry and Scott just stood there staring at him again.

"What?" Jimmy asked them and then headed off after Mary.

Henry and Scott looked at each other and they both smiled at the same time. Then they too started walking back to the clearing.

Behind them the small body settled more to the ground as the insects of the forest started to consume the corpse. The dead may be walking but to the insects of the world it was just another day.

They were all spread out once more in the small glade, catching a breather before they once again forged on. No one was talking as each of them was lost in their own thoughts.

Then Jimmy spoke up to break the silence. "I wonder what happened to my Dad when all this shit went down."

Nobody said anything as the statement hung in the air. Then Scott added:

"Yeah I know what you mean; my girlfriend lived a few streets over from where you guys picked me up. It's hard to imagine she's one of those things walking around out there."

Scott looked over at Mary and said: "Do you have any one you're worried about Mary?"

"You know I hate to say it but no. I mean not really. My family lives out of state and I was never really that close to anyone else." She hesitated for a moment.

"At least until I met you guys." She said smiling softly. Then the dog barked at her and her smile went from ear to ear as she rubbed the dog's head. "Yes big boy and you too."

"Emily was pretty much all I had." Henry whispered to the group.

They all sat there for awhile, thinking about the people they had known who were now gone. Until Jimmy broke the silence once again: "Hey guys look at the bright side of things." He said as he stood up and went into the middle of their little circle.

"What could possibly be the bright side to everything that's happened?" Mary asked.

"Well, now you've all got me." Jimmy said as he held his hands out in front of him.

He was immediately pelted with leaves and twigs as the others laughed and threw debris at him.

With the solemn mood broken the four companions gathered up their gear and continued on their journey.

Reaching the top of the latest embankment they were attempting to navigate, Henry was pleasantly surprised to see they had reached the end of their journey.

The forest ended abruptly about fifty yards away. The shrubs and foliage neatly trimmed back. Where the foliage ended a perfectly manicured lawn continued, wrapping around the building on all sides. Henry could see a couple of picnic tables peeking out the back side of the building. He could imagine employees in white lab coats sitting outside during lunch as they enjoyed Nature's beauty.

The building itself was unremarkable. It had a round circular driveway and the front was mostly glass, with the initials PL stenciled on the lower windows and doors.

"Well, what do you think?" Mary asked.

"About what," Henry replied looking perplexed.

"Will it do for our needs?"

Henry frowned. "It'll have to, come on, let's go, my feet are killing me."

Mary picked up a stick and threw it out in front of her. The dog shot off after it like a rocket, running across the field to retrieve it and then galloping back as fast as he could.

The two of them played this game all the way to the front doors, where the group stopped again to discuss what awaited them inside. Jimmy was the first to speak.

"When we enter the lobby they'll be two doors that each lead off to a hallway that go deeper into the building. The only other way out is the elevator, which is on the right when you enter the lobby from the outside. And there's a receptionist's desk in the middle of the floor."

"That's where I sit, or did sit, before everything went crazy yesterday." Mary said. "Jimmy, don't forget to tell them about the security doors." Mary prompted Jimmy.

"Oh yeah, right, the two doors that lead off the lobby are solid metal and you have to have a code card to get through them."

"Jimmy," Henry queried. "Do you have a code card to get through those doors?"

"Um, I had one, but when Dr. Martin attacked me I left it on the break room table. It's probably still in there."

"Who's Dr. Martin?" Scott asked, as he broke his silence.

Jimmy filled him in on what he did at Pineridge and who Dr. Martin was. Finishing the story with when he had barely escaped from Martin, and had saved Mary on the road leading out to the highway.

"And then we saw Henry on the highway and picked him up." Jimmy finished.

"All right," Henry spoke up. "If story time is over let's go inside and see what's there."

He punctuated his sentence by cocking the shotgun, and then turned around to open the doors.

With guns drawn the four of them entered the building.

CHAPTER 36

Henry entered the building first, followed by Jimmy, Mary, Scott and then Mary's dog, bringing up the rear. The dog's tale wagging behind him like it was playing a game.

The first thing they noticed upon entering the spacious room was the smell. Like bad meat being left outside to long. Sweeping left to right Henry took in the whole room. Clear. But then where the hell was that smell coming from?

Using his hands he pointed for Jimmy and Scott to fan out and go to the far left and right sides of the lobby and for Mary to stay put at the door as she had no weapon.

Henry walked up to the lobby desk to inspect it when the dog came over and started to growl.

He was growling at the desk.

Henry moved a little closer to lean over the desk when out jumped a zombie right at his face, Henry pushed at it as hard as he could, thrusting it away from him, it staggered backward for a moment, then started lurching forward again. Its legs not cooperating with what its brain wanted it to do. Before it could get any closer to him, Henry fired two shotgun blasts at it. The first blast chiseled the right side of its waist off, sending a mist of blood over the lobby. The second blast took out the left side of its waist, leaving a thin strip of meat in the middle of its body.

The zombie seemed to try to balance its upper body for a second, but then gravity took over and the top half of its body toppled over onto the lobby floor, the legs continuing to move forward for another step until they too toppled over. The zombie was still moving, now trying to drag it self around. Henry walked over to the desk, picked up the computer monitor and then brought it down on the zombie's head, crushing it to the floor with the sound of shattered glass from the face of the monitor.

His area was clear; looking over at Scott he could see that he was having a little trouble of his own. A zombie had been lurking by one of the big potted plants that were scattered around the edges of the lobby. It had startled Scott and had paralyzed him for a few precious moments before he came to his senses again. As it stumbled toward him, the limbs moved stiffly.

Scott aimed the Glock Henry had given him and shot it in the face.

The bullet went through its right eye, demolishing the socket and then continuing out the back of its head, spraying brains and bits of skull all over the glass behind it. The force of the bullet throwing it against the wall as it then slid down to lie still.

On the other side of the lobby Jimmy found the source of the odor permeating the lobby.

The corpse was lying on its side with most of its face gone. Maggots had started growing and were covering it from head to toe. The corpse's pants undulated with the movement underneath. Jimmy turned away and walked back to the middle of the room.

"That looks like all of them," Henry said.

"For now "Scott replied back.

"It's safe Mary." Henry said, waving her over.

Jimmy pointed to the metal doors. "Those lead into the building, the cafeteria and break room are down that way."

"Then that's where we're going, we need water and food, in that order and that's where we'll find it." Henry said turning towards the doors.

"But wait, we don't have pass cards to gain entry with," Mary called to him.

Henry turned and smiled, cocking the shotgun as he walked up to the doors and fired at the card reader point blank. "Card accepted, "he grinned.

Where the card reader once sat on the wall there was now a gaping hole that went through to the other side. Henry leaned against the wall to look through and nearly had his eyes poked out as a zombie stuck its hand through the hole seeking his flesh.

Henry jumped back startled; before he could do anything the black lab came up beside him and bit down on the zombies arm right behind the wrist, shaking its head. The labs teeth cut into the wrist, severing nerves and tendons. The hand went limp in its mouth. The lab didn't stop pulling until the flesh between wrist and hand was severed and then with a snap, the wrist broke off in the dog's mouth. The dog took its prize and went to Mary and sat at her feet, setting the hand down on the floor and wagging its tale like he had just retrieved a stick.

"Now that's something you don't see everyday," Jimmy said to Scott.

"Ya think?" Scott answered back and then walked over to Henry.

"What's the plan Henry?" Scott asked.

"How about I open the door and when that walking piece of shit comes out you blow its fucking head off."

"Now?"

"No time like the present, get your gun up, I'm gonna open it".

Scott backed up a little and stood in front of the doors. Jimmy had also come over and with a nod to both Henry and Scott signified that he was ready if things got hairy.

Henry grabbed the doors and looked at Scott. He started mouthing one, two, and on three Henry pulled the doors open. With the lock shorted it popped open and the zombie shot through the door, straight at Scott. Scott fired the gun but due too nerves wasn't exactly on target. The bullet just grazed the zombie's neck as it barreled into Scott, pushing him to the floor and landing on top of him. Scott saw the teeth coming towards his face and cringed with the expectation of pain.

Just before they would have sunk into his neck, ripping the life from him, they stopped in mid air an inch from his neck.

Then the zombie was pulled back like a bungee cord at the end of its limit as the teeth pulled away. When Scott could focus again he saw that Henry had grabbed it by its collar and had yanked it away from him, throwing it against the floor.

As the zombie landed hard on its back, Henry slammed the shotgun stock into its head, stunning it. The second blow crushed the forehead down to its nose and this time it lay still.

"Are you all right Scott?" Jimmy asked reaching down to help him up.

"Shit that was close, thanks Henry," Scott said, with a little tremor in his voice.

"No problem, glad I could help." Waving to Mary he said, "Come on Mary, why don't we let your new friend go first. He's a good point man. Just in case there are any more zombies in this end of the building."

Mary frowned, but did as requested. Walking towards the door the lab trotted at her heels.

With the dog in the lead, the four of them headed deeper into the building.

Within another section of the building Dr. Martin heard the commotion taking place in the lobby. Rising up from what was left of the corpse he had been feeding on he headed off in the direction of the lobby.

He was still hungry and fresh meat wasn't far away.

CHAPTER 37

THE BUILDING WAS quiet as the four of them wandered down the halls. Some of the rooms had corpses in them, with parts of their bodies having been eaten away. Flies were in abundance surrounding the bodies as the insects went about their business feeding on the corpses and laying eggs.

Henry tried to hide his disgust but the smell was overwhelming. As they passed by rooms with doors Henry would stop and close them to try to cut down on the stink coming off the bodies.

"You know, when we clear this place out we're going to have to clean this place up. It's going to get real ripe, real fast in here."

"Great, now I have to work in this dump for free." Jimmy quipped back to no one in particular.

They paused in the hallway when shuffling sounds could be heard coming from the direction of the cafeteria. The black lab growled, his ears going back against his head.

"What do you think?" Jimmy asked the group.

"I think we should make them come to us," Henry said. "I'm tired of these bastards popping up around every dark corner. I say make them come to us and then we'll blow the shit out of them."

Jimmy nodded as Henry's idea formed in his head.

"Sounds like a good idea, so how do we get them to come to us?" Scott asked.

"That's easy," Jimmy replied. "We're the bait."

Henry and Jimmy walked forward until they were about ten feet from the opening to the cafeteria.

While Scott and Mary hung back with 'blackie'—as Henry had silently named the pooch. He hadn't run the name by Mary yet, things had been moving to fast for such trivial things.

Henry started tapping his shotgun on the wall "Yoo-hoo, come and get it," he called.

Jimmy started whistling, the sound high and quick, like he was trying to get a friends attention at a crowded function. The two were making so much noise they almost didn't hear the two zombies, as they stumbled into the hall. The couple didn't look good, even for zombies. The one on the right was female and by the uniform she had on Henry and Jimmy could tell she had probably worked in the lunchroom. Her face was unrecognizable as most of her face was cooked off; when she had died she had passed out right into the deep fat fryer, although neither Henry nor Jimmy could have known that. The one on the left was male, he too was wearing a lunchroom uniform, but his face had scored lines going across its cheek and forehead and the meat surrounding these scores were burned to a crisp. Henry put two and two together and figured this poor bastard had passed out on the grill when he died and ended up becoming well done himself.

As the two zombies got closer Henry and Jimmy raised their weapons, each took the zombie on the side they were standing on. At a nod from Henry they both let loose, blowing the zombies down and finishing each one with a shot to the head.

Henry turned around to look at Mary and waved her forward.

"Ok guys, lets move, once we've cleared this place out we can rest.

The rest of the first floor was empty, either Jimmy was right and there weren't that many people working yesterday when the contaminated water started flowing through the building's pipes or the zombies had wandered away in search of better hunting once everyone had had been slaughtered.

Either way it meant that for the moment they could take a breather. Everyone gathered in a spacious office with Henry standing watch by the door. Just in case.

"Christ its feels good to sit down." Jimmy breathed with a big sigh as he threw himself onto the couch in the corner of the office.

Scott looked at Henry and smiled. "So how long do you think we can stay here?"

Henry considered the question before answering, "First we have to clear out the rest of the building, if there are anymore of those fuckers in here with us then they have to go. Then we can lock this place up tight so that nothing can get in. Then we should be able to relax for a little while until the government can come in and take control again."

"But where does that leave us?" Mary asked from behind the big desk in the middle of the room. She was sitting down with Blackie's head in her lap. She was slowly stroking his head as his tail wagged back and forth.

"You saw what happened at the barricade and then at the gas station, they're killing everybody whether they're contaminated or not. If they find us here, how are we going to stop them from killing us too?" She said with concern in her voice.

"Don't you worry about that, I've been racking my brain for a solution but for the moment I haven't figured it all out. So for now let's just concentrate on the problems at hand, namely clearing all the dead bastards out of here and sealing the building up. OK?" Henry said to the whole room.

Everyone nodded in agreement, for the moment placated.

"Great" Henry said, "Now will one of you please come here and relieve me so I can go take a piss?"

Jimmy laughed "Sure, I got it, go ahead." He said getting up and taking Henry's place by the door.

Henry walked down the hall to the bathrooms. As he rounded the corner in the hallway, he paused for a moment. Had he heard footsteps? He waited in the hallway, standing perfectly still. The only sound he could hear was the soft sound of his breathing and the echoes of his friends talking down the hall behind him.

He stood motionless for another minute, waiting to hear the noise again, but when nothing was forthcoming he shrugged and racked it up to nerves.

As he approached the bathroom doors he smiled to himself.

There were two doors in front of him, one for men and one for women. It didn't really seem to matter at the moment, so he went

Henry raised the shotgun, feeling vulnerable sitting on the toilet with his pants down by his ankles. But that couldn't be helped now.

He braced himself, hopefully ready for what ever came next.

Nothing happened. Who ever was out there wasn't moving; but just continued to stand perfectly still in front of his stall.

Should he make the first move? He was at a severe disadvantage as the stall door opened in.

Carefully without moving his feet he stood up and pulled up his pants, the task a hundred times more difficult with only one hand because he'd be dammed if he was going to put the shotgun down.

When his belt buckle finally slid into his pant loop he breathed a small sigh of relief. If he was going to die here and now in this room then at least his pants were on. He reached out to the latch on the door, slipping it out of its metal sheath, ready to fling open the door and blast whoever was there straight to hell. Unfortunately he never got the chance.

Just as his hand was getting ready to pull the door open it flew back at him. As the shotgun was knocked from his hand, it rebounded off the door and struck him in the head.

Stunned for a precious few seconds he barely had time to get his hands up in front of his body before the grunting, clawing zombie was on top of him trying to rip off his face. The zombie was now on top of Henry, its teeth desperately trying to sink into the soft flesh of his neck. And if that wasn't bad enough the stall door closed behind it as it climbed on top of him, locking them both in the stall.

Henry got his hands under its neck and pushed it off him, it didn't go very far as it's back slammed against the stall door. Then it was on him again. Henry punched it in the face and kicked it in the balls but nothing was slowing it down. When the zombie attacked him again his back was pushed against the flusher of the toilet, He screamed as it dug into his back. With one hand frantically keeping the zombie at bay his other hand reached around at the pain digging into his back . . . and found the pen he'd put in his pocket yesterday at the gas station. With a fumbling hand he desperately stuck his hand in his back pocket trying to get a grip on the pen. But with the zombie slavering at his face it was next to impossible. Finally he felt his hand wrap around the pen and he yanked it out and with one smooth motion jammed it into the zombie's left eye. The eye exploded inward ripping nerves and muscle as the pen continued through the skull until it pierced the brain. Henry pushed as hard as he could until there was nothing left of the pen showing in the eye socket but the clicker at its tip. The zombie shuddered as the pen punctured its brain. As the spark of re-life went out of the other eye it collapsed on top Henry.

Then the main door of the bathroom flew in with a crash, Henry could hear the voices of his friends calling to him.

"In here." He said hoarsely with the zombie lying on his chest. "Get this fuckin' thing off of me."

Jimmy and Scott were able to get the stall door open and drag the zombie off him. Henry's shirt was covered in the juices that leaked out of the zombie's eye socket. As Jimmy threw the body to the floor he gasped "Holy shit. It's Dr. Martin!"

"No shit, I don't give a fuck who he was, he was trying to fucking eat me."

"You all right?" Jimmy asked as he checked Henry with his eyes for any signs of damage.

"Yeah, I think so, right now I just want to lie down." He said leaving the bathroom and going to an office to rest for awhile; the ordeal taking more of a toll on him than he wanted to admit to himself.

Scott retrieved the shotgun from the floor, and he and Jimmy walked out together.

Jimmy paused at the door and looked back at the zombie who was once Dr. Martin and said "Wow, I guess he wasn't such a dork after all."

Then he hit the light switch and closed the door, leaving the bathroom in darkness once more.

CHAPTER 39

H ENRY WAS DREAMING. He had just returned home from work after another long day. The house was quiet. The clock on the kitchen wall read 9:45. He went upstairs to take a shower, but before heading into the bathroom he peeked around the bedroom door to check on Emily. She was sleeping quietly, her chest rising and falling with an even rhythm. Their pet cat was curled up by her feet. He went into the bathroom and did the nightly chores people do all over the world every night. Finishing in the bathroom he went back downstairs to grab something to eat and watch some television.

When the news show he was watching ended he decided it was time to go to bed. Looking at the clock on the mantle he could see it was almost midnight.

He quietly went up the stairs and climbed into bed next to his wife. He curled up close to her under the bed covers and caressed her body. Even after twenty-one years together she still excited him.

She didn't stir as he entered her, her breathing never changing. He continued to make love to her for another five minutes until he felt he was going to explode. Then when he couldn't stand it anymore he pulled out of her and ejaculated on the sheets. Feeling good after the sexual release he turned over and relaxed before he knew he'd have to get up and clean up his little mess or Emily would kill him.

Emily groaned next to him, he couldn't see her face as she was lying on her side. Then she made a gargling noise and Henry started to get worried. He tried to shake her awake but it wasn't working so he leaned over and turned on the bedside light to see if she was okay. He rolled her onto her back and was horrified to see she was dead. But not just dead, she was dead and rotting.

Her face was like dried leather and as he watched a maggot wiggled out of her ear and dropped to the sheet. Her cheeks were undulating as thousands of maggots squirmed under the skin, then before his eyes the skin on her face started ripping open from the inside out. The maggots shot out of her face as if propelled and landed onto Henry's face. He started screaming as they started crawling into his nose and mouth, he could feel them crawling on his eyeballs and under his eyelids.

He kept screaming and screaming until he felt he couldn't take it anymore.

Then he felt himself being shaken like a rag doll and he opened his eyes and Jimmy was standing over him.

"Henry? Jesus man, I've been shaking you for like five fucking minutes; that must have been some dream you were having." Jimmy said with his hands still holding Henry's shoulders.

"What? Yeah, I guess so, to tell you the truth I really don't remember much about it, though I think it freaked me the hell out." He said still drowsy from sleep.

Jimmy let him go. "Listen, me and Scott were gonna go check the other side of the building for any more of those zombie fuckers."

"Yeah? You want me to come along?" Henry asked, slurring his words a little.

"No it's cool, we should be able to handle it, but ah, can I use your shotgun? I'll leave the Glock with you instead." Jimmy said with expectation.

"Sure Jimmy go ahead, but be careful, and remember, let them come to you."

"You bet Henry, we'll be back before you know it."

With that said Jimmy headed out of the room to grab Scott and go do a little hunting.

Henry laid back down still tired, thinking to himself that he'd never get back to sleep after the dream he just had, and without even realizing it he was out again moments later.

Thankfully, this time no dreams came to him.

CHAPTER 40

JIMMY AND SCOTT walked through the lobby on their way to the elevator. Their mood was cheerful; the two of them acting like two kids who were able to do something alone without their parent's supervision.

Jimmy was a little ahead of Scott and was the first one to the elevator. He pressed the button and together they waited for the elevator doors to open. The bell chimed the arrival of the elevator, the doors opened and to both men's surprise a body fell out. Jimmy had to jump back so that the corpse didn't land on him.

"What the fuck?" Jimmy yelled.

"Oh wow man that guy is seriously dead." Scott said, while studying the body.

"You think?" Jimmy said back sarcastically.

From a closer examination the two men concluded that the now dead man on the lobby floor had been attacked somewhere else and must have made it to the elevator before bleeding out all over the elevator car's floor. They picked him up and together they dragged him to the front door, where they tossed him outside in the driveway.

"Ashes to ashes, "Scott said before they walked back inside.

"Dust to dust," Jimmy finished.

Once back inside they boarded the elevator and headed up to the second floor. During the ride up both men tried to ignore the fact that the floor was painted red with blood, the congealing blood sticking to their shoes as they moved about on the floor.

When the elevator chimed the arrival to the second floor both men had their guns drawn.

"Let's stay here and give a yell, if anything comes at us we can always close the doors and head back down." Jimmy suggested.

"Or we'll be trapped in a 4x4 box with zombies trying to eat our asses off." Scott sniped back.

"I like my idea better. You ready?"

"Yeah, I guess so. Let's do this so we can go back down. It's so empty up here, it gives me the creeps." Scott said.

Jimmy started banging on the wall with his hands and kicking the doors with his feet while yelling up a storm. It didn't take long before one of the zombies on the floor heard them and started walking in their direction. The walking corpse turned into the hallway right into the sights of Scott and Jimmy.

"Oh fuck here comes one Jimmy, whose gonna shoot it, you or me?"

"Go ahead Scott blow it's fucking head off." Jimmy smiled at him.

Scott raised the Glock in front of him and lined up the zombie and fired. The first shot hit it in the stomach. It lurched back for a second then continued on, the bullet barely slowing it down.

"In the head Scott, shoot it in the fucking head." Jimmy yelled at him.

Scott nodded once then lined up the zombie's head with the barrel of his gun and fired.

This time his aim was true, the shell entered the zombie's nose, going straight through into the skull where it then exploded out the back of the zombie's head, taking most of the skull bone with it. The zombie dropped to the floor with a dull thud.

"Yeah!" Scott yelled. "Got him."

"All right, all right, don't get cocky, there's probably more of them up here, so stay sharp." Jimmy chastised him.

The two of them started banging and yelling again. After about five minutes had passed and nothing had stirred in the hallway; so they decided to give up on drawing the zombies out.

"Well Scott, what do you think, maybe that's all of them?"

"No way, Jimmy, there's got to be more than one on this floor. We're gonna have to go in after the dead fuckers. Come on."

With that said Scott headed down the hallway. Jimmy paused for a second and then followed him as well, mumbling under his breath.

"Shit it would have been nice if there was only one." He said.

As they came upon the first office door Jimmy went to the left side and Scott to the right. With a nod from Jimmy, Scott kicked the door in.

Two female zombies came charging out of the room. As Scott was directly in their path they both went at him.

The first one got a bullet in the neck for its trouble as it dived at Scott. The wound didn't stop it but it did throw it off balance enough for Scott to sidestep it. The second one never got near Scott. Before it was close enough to do any harm Jimmy broke its head in with the stock of the shotgun. The zombie dropped to the floor and lay still. The one Scott had shot had regained its balance and was now reaching for Scott again. Scott raised his gun and put a bullet straight through her mouth; the bullet ricocheted off her teeth and then exited out her cheek.

She now had a hole in the side of her face big enough to see the inside of her mouth. Her tongue, now swollen from death flopped out of the hole and writhed back and forth.

"Holy shit is that gross." Jimmy said as he watched the zombie.

Then he brought up the shotgun and pulled the trigger. But he squeezed too quickly and instead of the head being shot the barrage of bullets took her neck out, severing the head from its shoulders in one shot.

The head seemed to float in the air for a micro second, as if it didn't realize its neck was gone. Then the head tumbled to the floor where the zombie's foot kicked it down the hallway. Then the zombie toppled over onto the other one and lay still as well.

"Jesus, Scott, did you see that? Zombie head soccer; and I'd thought I'd seen everything." Jimmy said trying to break his freaked out mood. He was really more shaken up than he wanted to admit.

Scott just looked at Jimmy; still way to freaked to do more than nod.

The two men continued down the hallway checking rooms as they went, when they arrived at the copy room Jimmy paused and looked at Scott.

"I'll go in first, you get my back." Jimmy told Scott.

Scott nodded and followed behind him.

When Jimmy walked into the room he could immediately smell death. Either there was something in here with them or something had died in here recently and was rotting somewhere nearby. The two men scanned the room. There were two copy machines, one on each side of the room and a desk in the middle where the clerks or lab assistants could lay out the work they needed to copy.

The table had a frilly white table cloth that hanged down to the floor.

Jimmy looked at Scott and pointed to him to go check the supply closet at the back of the room. Scott frowned, but did as he was asked. He crept over to the open closet door and slowly poked his head in, ready to pull it back if something tried to grab him.

The closet was empty. He breathed a sigh of relief and then nodded no to Jimmy.

Jimmy signed him 'ok' with his hand and then pointed that they should leave.

As Jimmy was turning around to leave the room a hand reached out from under the table and pulled his legs out from under him.

Jimmy went flying backwards and hit his head on the copy machine. Dazed for a moment he wasn't able to defend himself from the zombie that was now climbing up his body.

Jimmy shook his head, trying to clear it, and in a moment was a little more clearheaded. Just as the zombie was ready to rip out his neck Jimmy took a fist and punched the zombie under the chin. The zombies jaw slammed closed with a thwack, as the teeth cut off the tip of its tongue. As the zombies head rocked back Jimmy got his arms under it and pushed it off. The zombie flew across the room but was charging back at Jimmy in moments. Jimmy sidestepped it and pushed it to the floor.

"What do you want me to do?" Scott yelled while waving his gun around, not wanting to shoot for fear of hitting Jimmy.

Jimmy realized this too and yelled at Scott. "Don't you do shit, I got this, put that gun away before you shoot me with it."

Jimmy watched the zombie with a wary eye. Now that Jimmy was on his feet again he could see he had at least a hundred pounds on the zombie in front of him. The zombie couldn't have weighed more than a hundred pounds even at the best of times. And now wasn't the best of times for the animated corpse.

Jimmy decided to have a little fun with this one. After all it would be nice to be on the giving end for a change.

"Scott, watch the door and make sure we don't get any unwelcome visitors.

I'm gonna have a little fun with this one first."

Scott sighed but did as requested of him. "Fine Jimmy, but don't take too long ok?"

Jimmy nodded and then turned his full attention to the zombie with a gleam in his eye.

The zombie lunged at Jimmy again but this time Jimmy was ready for it. He sidestepped its charge and then got its head in a headlock. The zombie kicked and grabbed but didn't have the raw power to escape.

Then Jimmy dragged it over to the copy machine and opened the cover with his free hand. He hit the power button and slammed the zombies face into the glass.

Then he hit print, the light came on and started scanning the zombie's face, as printed copies started falling into the bin on the side of the copier.

As the scanner kept going the glass started getting hotter and hotter. Soon the smell of burning meat filled the room as the zombie's face was melting to the glass.

Scott wrinkled his face in disgust and covered his nose.

"Come on man that's enough. Finish the little bastard so we can get out of here.

Jimmy looked at Scott and even though he still wanted to keep going he nodded to Scott.

"Ok Scott, for you, anything," Jimmy sneered at him.

Jimmy then stood back and let the zombie go and retrieved his shotgun from the floor. The zombie stood up from the copy machine, the left side of its face tearing off and staying on the glass. The skin had melted to the glass from the heat of the scanner. As the zombie stood up the copier got each disgusting second recorded as the side of its face ripped off.

The zombie turned around to lunge at Jimmy again, but Jimmy was ready as he stood there with his legs spread wide for balance and fired the shotgun point blank at the zombie's head. The head was blown apart, pieces of it landing on the hot glass of the copier and steaming from the heat.

Scott turned his head in disgust as Jimmy walked over to the copier and retrieved the copies of the zombies face.

He looked at them for a moment and said: "Hey you know what? This new ink does give better quality pictures."

He handed them to Scott smiling and said. "Here you go Scott, for your

Memoirs," and then walked out the door.

Scott stood in the doorway for a moment and stared at the papers in his hand. Then he threw them down onto the floor where they covered the zombie from head to toe. Then he closed the door and left.

The search continued, but not with much luck, though neither was complaining. They had to go door to door with the expectation that around the next door would be a hungering fiend out for their blood. They'd get all pumped up as they got to a door, fingers ready on triggers only to kick the door in and find an empty office or lab. Sometimes they'd find a dead body. Usually, most of it would be eaten away. It looked like they had gotten them all until in one of the offices they found a zombie in the corner in a wheelchair.

"Oh shit," Jimmy gasped. "I know this guy."

"You did?" questioned Scott.

"Yeah, I use to see him out side at the picnic tables sometimes. He was cool; if he saw me he would always say hi, not like some of those other assholes who worked here.

"You want to do it?" Scott asked handing the Glock to Jimmy "Here use mine; don't waste the shotgun on it. Just do it quick will you? No games this time."

"Jimmy traded guns with Scott and walked over to the wheelchair. The zombie's arms reached out to grab him but he just sidestepped out of its way and walked behind it. The zombie tried to turn around but the chair wouldn't let it. Making sure Scott wasn't going to get sprayed with blood Jimmy put the gun to the zombie's head and squeezed. The bullet took half its head off and the zombie sagged in the chair.

Jimmy was just about to say something to Scott when two more zombies appeared in the doorway, right where Scott was standing.

"Scott, watch out!" Jimmy warned him. But it was too late.

Before Jimmy could even get his weapon up the two zombies had Scott in a death grip and were bringing him down to the floor.

Before Scott's body had even hit the floor the zombie on his right had sunk his teeth into his neck and severed the jugular. Scott tried to scream but the blood was choking him as it ran down his throat and into his lungs, drowning him in his own blood.

Jimmy jumped forward and hit the nearest zombie in the face with the barrel of his gun. As that one fell back he grabbed the shotgun off the floor where Scott had dropped it and stuck it in the other zombie's face and pulled the trigger. The zombies head didn't just disintegrate, no, it was more like one second the head was sitting on its shoulders and the next second after the blast it wasn't. The other zombie had started to rise by now and Jimmy swiveled on his boots and shot it point blank in the chest. The force of the blast actually sent the zombie sliding across the floor a few feet. Its chest was a heaving mass of exposed meat. As it tried to get up again its insides poured out, after being pulverized by the shotgun blast. Screaming, Jimmy ran over to it and shot it in the face. The body flew back and hit the floor like it had been pushed over, and landed minus a face. It didn't move again.

Jimmy ran over to Scott to see how he was. "Scott, speak to me, don't worry buddy, you're gonna be ok." He said while cradling him in his arms. Jimmy's shirt was immediately soaked in blood from Scott's wound.

Scott looked up into Jimmy's eyes. He tried to say something but the blood in his throat made it just sound like gargling sounds.

"Scott, Scott, come on man stay with me. You're not gonna die. I won't let you. With that Scott's eyes glazed over as he succumbed to blood loss.

Jimmy sat there with Scott cradled in his arms for what seemed like a very long time, then he got up, collected his weapons and went back downstairs to tell the others what had happened.

Jimmy entered the elevator and pressed the lobby button. As the doors closed, blocking Jimmy's view of Scott, a single tear rolled down his cheek. Jimmy wasn't concerned; he knew there'd be more to come.

CHAPTER 41

MARY WAS IN the lobby playing with Blackie. His name was now official after Henry had talked with her about his suggestion for a name. She was throwing a plastic dinner plate she had found in one of the offices. Blackie was having fun running around the lobby, trying to catch the plate and then trotting back to her with it stuck in his mouth.

She had heard the muffled gun shots upstairs and hoped Jimmy and Scott were all right. A few more minutes passed as she kept playing with Blackie.

That's when she heard the elevator chime. She turned to see who it was when Jimmy walked out covered in blood.

"Oh my god Jimmy, are you all right?" She asked while running over to him.

"Relax Mary, I'm fine, it's not my blood on my shirt. Where's Henry?" he asked.

"He's doing inventory of our water and food. He just started a few minutes ago. "Why, Jimmy, where's Scott?"

Jimmy just looked at her, and then went to find Henry.

Henry had just finished counting the water they had available. Counting the bottles from the vending machines they should be fine for at least a week, maybe more if they rationed a little.

Food would last longer as they had the cafeteria freezer and the vending machines to keep them fed. He was just about to start a loose inventory of their food stores when he heard Jimmy calling his name.

He headed out into the hallway and almost walked right into him. Jimmy looked a mess, his shirt was covered in blood and he had a frazzled look about him. Henry was pretty sure there'd been trouble upstairs.

"What's wrong? Any problems upstairs?" he asked Jimmy.

"Yeah I guess you could say that. We got cornered and two zombies got the jump on Scott, it all happened so fast, he never had a chance." Jimmy looked down at the floor. "He's dead Henry."

Henry just stood there; it felt like someone had just punched him in the gut. He didn't know what to do or say. He just stood there in shock.

Mary came down the hallway with Blackie in tow. She had tears in her eyes. "He's dead isn't he?" She asked Henry.

"Yes he is Mary, Jimmy just filled me in."

Jimmy had tears in his eyes. "So what do we do now?"

Henry sighed" Well, we'll bury him, I guess."

"When do you want to do it" Jimmy asked Henry.

"The sooner the better." Mary jumped in. Then she started to cry again.

Henry went to her and put his arm around her. She turned and buried her face into his chest.

They stood there for a while until she got control of herself.

"You stay down here and keep an eye on things; me and Jimmy will go get Scott."

She nodded and walked back into the office, the dog still right behind her.

Henry turned and walked out to the lobby. Jimmy was waiting there for him. As Henry approached he handed Henry back the shotgun.

"Thanks, this helped a lot."

"Obviously not enough" Henry said with utterly no malice in his voice but just stating a fact.

They got onto the elevator and road up in silence, the elevator chimed its arrival and the two stepped off the elevator. To see a third zombie feeding on Scott, ripping his stomach open to get at his organs. As the two walked out the zombie paid them no attention. It had its meat and for the time being was content. Jimmy walked up to it with purpose in his stride and put the gun to its head and pulled the trigger. With its brains blown onto the adjacent wall it fell on top of Scott and lay still.

"Bastards," Jimmy muttered "No good fucking bastards."

With that said he kicked the zombie in the gut, the corpse shifting slightly from the impact.

Henry walked up behind him and put his hand on Jimmy's shoulder.

"Come on Jimmy," he whispered, "Lets clean this floor of any more of those bastards before we get Scott, that way we don't have to keep looking over our shoulders."

Jimmy nodded, his eyes never leaving Scott's body. Then he turned and the two of them went hunting one final time.

CHAPTER 42

THE SUN WAS setting behind the three people standing quietly over an unmarked grave. The darkness slowly descended around them, each one of them lost in his or her private thoughts.

Henry was thinking back to just a few hours ago. After Jimmy had killed the zombie who had been feeding on Scott the two of them had continued searching the second floor for any more.

They had found another seven or eight—Henry wasn't really sure as he wasn't keeping count-scattered around the floor hiding in the other rooms. One they had found trapped in a private bathroom.

The person had evidently died inside the room and then couldn't get out after he had reanimated.

Jimmy had found it actually, he had just wanted to take a piss and as he opened the door the zombie had jumped out at him. It hadn't fed since it had come back to life and was ravenous. The zombie had wrestled Jimmy to the ground before Henry could get his gun up. Jimmy was on his back trying to keep its jaws from taking a bite out of him.

"Shoot it for Christ sake!" Jimmy screamed.

Henry couldn't shoot without hitting Jimmy as they were rolling around on the floor and Henry couldn't get a good shot.

Henry turned the shotgun around and held the barrel like a baseball bat, then swung at the zombies head like he played for the Majors. The gunstock hit the zombie's head with a cracking sound, the head leaning to the side with the force of the blow. Bone showed through as the gunstock ripped the skin. Its grip on Jimmy loosened enough for Jimmy to get his legs under its body and kick it off him. The corpse flew across the floor and landed back inside the bathroom. Henry quickly reached over and shut the door. He then quickly grabbed a small wooden chair and placed it under the doorknob of the door. The door was now jammed shut.

As the zombie pounded on the door to get out the door shook on its hinges.

Henry took a deep breath as he reached down to help Jimmy back up.

"Shit that was close, another second and you would have been planting me next to Scott." Jimmy gasped, trying to get his breath back.

"Well that didn't happen, and it won't happen, you hear me Jimmy." Henry's eyes stared straight at Jimmy's, never wavering or blinking. After a few seconds Jimmy looked away, breaking eye contact. "Yeah Henry ok, I get it, its not gonna happen."

"Good, now if you're ready lets finish this floor and attend to Scott." With that Henry turned and walked out of the room and back into the hall.

Jimmy thought about what he had just said to Henry "Not gonna happen." He muttered to himself.

"I sure fucking hope not." He said, and then he followed Henry back into the hall to take care of business.

Behind them the trapped zombie continued to bang on the door.

Henry was the first to break the silence that was surrounding them as they stood around Scott's grave.

"I'd like to say something if it's all right," Henry said quietly.

Jimmy and Mary both nodded yes.

"I didn't know Scott that well, but what I did know was that he was a good man. I felt safe knowing he had my back. We've all lost a lot of people in the past two days and as we ourselves try to survive this hell we've been thrown into. I hope we can all live up to Scott's courage and bravery."

"Amen, "Mary whispered at his side.

"Yeah, Henry that was nice, I think Scott would have liked it." Jimmy added.

Jimmy looked down at the mound of dirt. "Goodbye buddy, I'm so sorry this happened."

With that said Jimmy turned and headed back inside. Mary started to go after him, but stopped when she felt Henry's hand on the side of her arm.

"Let him go Mary, just give him a few minutes alone."

Mary nodded, assenting to his request. Darkness surrounded them like a shroud as the two people stood quietly together once more, lost in their private thoughts.

CHAPTER 43

JIMMY WAS THE first back into the lobby, as he entered he could hear a distant thumping coming from upstairs on the second floor. He ignored it and walked over to the desk in the middle of the room. He kept going over the events leading up to Scott's death, trying to make some sense of it all, but the truth was there wasn't any. In this new world they had been thrust into people died. Shit, a lot of people died. He'd probably die too. How long could he keep out running death before it finally caught up to him? When would his luck run out?

He heard the elevator door ping and tensed as he turned to see it opening on its own. He waited quietly for someone or something to come out. When a few tense moments passed with no results, he walked over to investigate with his hand on his gun; ready to pull it out at a hint of danger.

"Empty? What the hell?" He mumbled to himself.

He looked up as Mary and Henry came through the lobby door and then walked up to stand beside him.

Mary saw him at the elevator door and queried him about it.

"Hey, Jimmy. Did the elevator open on its own again?"

"Yeah," Jimmy replied. "It was the funniest thing."

"Not really," Mary smiled back. "It does that every now and then. I asked one of the repair men one time and he says it has something to do with it cycling through its program something or other. Either way I know it always does it when it sits too long without use.

Then they all heard the muffled banging coming from above again.

Henry cocked his ear while looking at the ceiling, "You know we're gonna have to take care of that sooner or later." He said pointing at the ceiling.

"I know, but how about later? It's trapped and even if it got out its still up there and we're down here."

"Yeah, we'll do it later. Look it's late, what do you say we lock this place down and get some rest? I'm exhausted."

"Yeah me too, I didn't realize how much until you just said it." She said while uncoiling her arms in a stretch.

"It'll be nice to sleep on something other than a minivan seat." Mary finished as she turned and started walking down the hall to the offices.

"Yeah, I'm pretty wasted too, all right lets go. You coming Henry?" Jimmy said.

"You go ahead, I'm just gonna lock up down here first." Henry said as he walked back to the lobby doors to secure them for the night.

When the doors were secured he went over to the elevator and pressed the call button. When the door opened Henry took a potted plant from the lobby and stuck it in between the frame so the elevator wouldn't close. Then he looked up at the ceiling. "Better safe then sorry." he mumbled to himself.

Then he headed down the hallway to join the others for the night.

As the companions slept that night the zombie continued to bang on the door, slowly weakening the hinges from its body weight. The vibration of the door soon shook the chair loose and it fell with a dull clatter onto the short weaved rug.

The banging continued long into the night.

CHAPTER 44

JIMMY WAS DREAMING. In his dream he was running; from what he wasn't sure. He just new he had to escape before it reached him.

He was running through the woods. The moon was full in the sky overhead. The moonlight shined down through the trees and gave everything a yellow tint. He was running flat out, headless of the obstacles in his path. The branches ripped his clothes and scratched his face. He didn't care.

All he knew was that he had to get away. Get away before it caught him.

He had never felt terror like this before, a fear so deep in his soul he thought his heart would explode from the inability to contain it.

So he ran.

Shapes started appearing in his peripheral vision as he ran through the trees. Shadowy figures that disappeared when he turned his head towards them, trying to get a better look.

The path in the woods started to ascend. He followed it up, constantly looking over his shoulder, waiting for the hand of death to touch him.

As he neared the top a shape began to form out of the air in front of him. The closer he got the clearer it became, until Jimmy could see it was a person. The face was shrouded in darkness.

When Jimmy reached the top, the figure stood before him and raised its arms out wide.

Jimmy stared with his mouth open as the figure's face became revealed.

It was Scott.

But now he was a zombie.

Scott's eyes were missing, in their place hundreds of maggots squirmed and danced in the reflection of the moonlight. The front of his chest was a gaping, raw wound. Rats scurried about inside his body, poking their heads out to rip a piece of meat off the edges of the wound and then disappearing back inside.

Scott opened his mouth to speak. His voice sounding like his throat was full of crushed glass. "You killed me Jimmy," Scott said. "You left me to die."

"No!" Jimmy screamed, "It wasn't my fault you died! I'm sorry Scott!"

Jimmy fell to his knees. Tears were coming down his face. "I'm so fuckin sorry," he cried.

Zombie Scott walked closer to Jimmy, cupping Jimmy's face in its skeletal hands. "Apology not accepted," it growled.

Then his hands wrapped around Jimmy's face, the thumbs pushing into his eyes. Scott pressed until Jimmy's eyes were a bloody pulp, the mess of blood and fluid ran down Jimmy's face and into the dirt.

Jimmy started to scream.

Jimmy could feel the thumbs pushing past his eye sockets and into his brain.

He screamed again, and continued screaming until his vocal chords were raw.

Then he woke up. He immediately felt his eyes, expecting them to be nothing but empty sockets. Relief flooded through him as he realized that he was intact and had just had a nightmare.

Already the nightmare was whisking away from his conscious thought.

He checked his watch and realized it was almost daybreak so he got up and went to the bathroom to attend to nature and then went down to the cafeteria to get something to eat.

The cafeteria was nothing more than a standard house kitchen set into the room it now occupied.

With a few extras added like a small steam table and vending machines.

Jimmy grabbed a bottle of milk out of the refrigerator, admiring Henry's handiwork organizing the water and some of the food. There was a box of cookies on top of the refrigerator as well, so he grabbed those and made a meal out of it.

He had finished his meal and had just started cleaning up his mess when Mary walked in.

Her eyes were half closed and clearly she wasn't fully awake.

"Hey Jimmy," she asked "if you're up would you bring Blackie outside so he can go to the bathroom? He's driving me crazy."

"Sure Mary, I could use some fresh air anyway," Jimmy said. "Come on boy; let's go outside for a walk."

Jimmy and Blackie headed out to the lobby, Jimmy paused a moment; he could still hear a dull thumping, although it did appear to be slowing down. Jimmy smiled when he saw the elevator propped open, he'd have to comment on that to Henry when he saw him later in the morning.

Unlocking the lobby doors he let Blackie out to run around and go to the bathroom. He felt confident that he was safe. If anything was out there in the woods and got to close to him the dog would give him a sign.

The woods were quiet with just a hint of sunrise coming to the sky. Jimmy felt a chill as a small part of his nightmare flashed through his mind.

Shaking it off Jimmy wandered around the grounds, following Blackie as he explored his new home.

Blackie went over to the pile of corpses that Henry and Scott had made after cleaning out the building. They would burn them tomorrow in daylight so the fire wouldn't be too noticeable.

Jimmy shooed him away from the pile as the flies were everywhere, he didn't need the dog getting sick from the decomposing bodies.

Jimmy had taken a seat on one of the benches and was stretching out to relax when Blackie started barking.

"What is it boy, what's the matter?" Jimmy asked the dog.

Blackie ignored him and continued to bark, now alternating with growls.

"Come on boy, I think its time we go back inside." He said as he started to back up; he was getting a really bad feeling.

As he turned around he caught a glimpse of something coming at him from his right side.

A zombie had snuck up on him. Dammit, he had dropped his guard for one minute and now it might be his last. There was no one out here to help him. Even if he yelled for help his friends wouldn't hear his cries inside the building. And he had left his gun inside as well.

Cursing his stupidity, he started backing away from it. This one was a big bastard Jimmy noticed.

One of its eyes appeared to be moving in its socket like it had a life of its own. Then as the shadows retreated from its face Jimmy could see that the eye was missing and that what he saw was an undulating mass of maggots inside the eye socket of its head. He shivered as a part of his nightmare flashed in his mind.

As Jimmy backed away he noticed the zombie had to turn its head more to compensate for the impaired vision. That might help him, Jimmy thought.

The zombie had to be at least 6'1. It had shoulders like a lumberjack. If this thing got a hold of him, Jimmy knew he'd never be able to escape its grip. The zombie's bigger legs also gave it a wider walking radius: this guy moved fast. Jimmy looked where the lobby doors were and knew he'd never make it before it was on him. All the while Blackie was barking at it and biting its legs.

The zombie wasn't even slowing down. Jimmy felt panic rising in his gut and fought to keep it down. If he lost his head then he was dead meat.

Jimmy looked on his left and could see Scott's grave, he felt a pang of sadness, even as he realized he'd be joining him in a minute or two. Then his eyes spotted a glint of metal as the sun was coming up. The shovel they had used to bury Scott was still at the grave. Jimmy bolted at a run to grab the shovel with the zombie only a few feet behind, if he tripped on a root or fell in a gopher hole he'd be ripped apart seconds after his body landed on the ground.

Jimmy arrived at the grave and grabbed the shovel and swung it in one motion. The zombie was struck in the chest, the blow barely phasing it. Jimmy started backing up with the shovel in front of him, trying to fend off the creature's flailing arms and hands.

Jimmy started sliding over to the zombie's blind side, and as the zombies head overcompensated Jimmy dove in and slammed the shovel into its face, then quickly pulled back. It staggered for a moment and then continued after Jimmy; now with a crushed nose.

"It's like fucking Davy and Goliath with this guy." He muttered to himself, swinging the shovel back and forth. "And I'm Davy."

He was now getting close to the end of the grassy area of the grounds, the trees closing in on him and making it harder to swing the shovel. He now had to be careful not to trip over anything while walking backwards through the woods. His arms were getting tired and he knew he wouldn't be able to keep this up for much longer.

Then he caught a glimpse of two tree trunks that had grown into a V.

The tree's bottoms were together and the trunks had gradually grown apart.

Jimmy got an idea, he started backing towards the malformed tree with the zombie following, gaining ground on him with every step it made. When Jimmy reached the trees he turned sideways and hopped between the two trunks. The zombie followed but due to its wider shoulders got stuck.

Jimmy only had seconds before the hulking zombie freed itself and continued the chase.

That was all Jimmy needed; the second his shoulders had cleared the trees he had pivoted on his heels and raised the shovel over his head like he was chopping wood. Then he brought the shovel down onto the zombie's head with as much force his whole body could put in to it.

The shovel connected with the zombie's forehead with such force that the skull cracked like Jimmy had just hit a watermelon. Blood and brains flew in all directions, splashing on Jimmy and Blackie. The zombie stopped moving but stayed where it was, its shoulders still wedged in between the two trees. With a deep breath Jimmy looked at the dog. "Shit, Blackie some help you were."

The dog just stared at him as it cocked its head to the side, as if he knew what Jimmy was saying.

Jimmy stepped back a little further from the zombie, just to make sure it was dead. Then he turned and started walking back to Pineridge.

"Come on boy, let's get back inside." He said, slapping the side of his leg for the dog to follow. Blackie barked once and then trotted after him.

Behind them the zombie slipped from the tree and fell to the ground.

Jimmy turned around startled but quickly relaxed a little when he pieced together what had happened.

Jimmy looked at Blackie. "Tell me boy, does a zombie make a sound when it falls in the forest if there's no one around to hear it?"

The dog just stared at him. Jimmy then turned back around and continued back to Pineridge.

His arms were so sore he dragged the shovel behind him all the way back to the building, with the shovelhead bouncing behind him.

In the sky overhead the sun had finished rising, it was going to be a beautiful day.

CHAPTER 45

MARY HAD JUST finished making coffee and had poured herself the first cup. Then she had walked out into the lobby and sat down at her desk. It was silly she new but with all the craziness going on around her it felt safe and familiar to sit there.

After Jimmy had agreed to take Blackie for a walk she had gone back to the office she had called home for the night.

As she lay back down to try to go back to sleep she found that she couldn't. Yesterday's events kept intruding on her thoughts and no matter how hard she tried she couldn't put them out of her mind.

Finally she gave up and had decided to go to the kitchen.

Now as she sat at her desk she started to wonder where Jimmy and Blackie were. They had been outside for at least a half an hour now and she was getting a little worried.

After all, they were miles away from anybody, how dangerous could it be out there?

The thumping was still going on over her head, although more sporadically now than last night.

She was just about to go wake Henry up and ask him to check on Jimmy when the doors to the lobby opened and in walked Jimmy and Blackie.

Neither of them looked the way they had when they had set out for their walk a little earlier that morning.

Jimmy was panting heavily, his face streaked with blood. His shirt was filthy, grass stains completely covered it and there were little bits of what appeared to be meat all over him.

Blackie trotted over to her and she could see he too had streaks of red on his black coat and there was a hint of red on the corner of the dog's mouth.

"Oh my god, what happened to the two of you? Are you all right?"

"We're fine Mary, nothing to worry about. Is Henry up yet?" He asked her.

"I don't think so, but you could check."

"That's okay, I think I'll go lay back down again. I'm feeling pretty wasted."

"Ok, I'll see you when you get back up later."

Jimmy headed back down the hall to his bed.

"Jimmy?" Mary called after him. Jimmy turned to look at her."Yeah?" He asked "What happened out there?" She inquired again.

"What happened was I got lucky," he said to her, as if that had answered her question.

She just smiled back. "Ok Jimmy, You don't have to tell me if you don't want to. I'm just glad you're ok."

"Yeah," he said. "Me too." Then he turned and headed back to bed.

Mary watched Blackie as he ran around the lobby. He sure wasn't acting like a dog that had just been outside exercising. In fact he looked more wound up than before he went outside.

"All right boy, I'll play with you." She said as she picked up the dinner plate and threw it for him to catch. This went on for the next ten minutes and Mary was getting bored with the game.

On her latest throw she didn't pay attention where she was throwing the disc and it accidentally landed in the elevator, which was still propped open by the plant Henry had placed there last night.

Blackie plowed into the elevator to retrieve his toy and knocked the plant stand out of the frame. The elevator doors closed immediately as it cycled through its programming. Blackie started to bark as the doors closed and jumped up against the buttons. His paws pressed the second floor button and the elevator began to ascend.

In moments the elevator opened on the second floor and Blackie charged out, glad to be free again. Once out he stopped to explore his new surroundings, his nose picking up the scent of death left over from the zombies the men had killed a day earlier.

Then Blackie heard a muffled banging coming from down the hall.

The dog's ears perked up as he zeroed in on the direction of the sound and then he shot off down the hallway to investigate.

His long toenails clicked on the polished floor as he ran down the hallway, searching for the origination of the muffled banging.

Mary watched as Blackie charged into the elevator to fetch his toy and was annoyed when the doors shut on her dog.

"Great," she said as she stood up to go release him.

When she arrived at the elevator she was surprised to see it had gone upstairs. Quickly she pressed the call button and while tapping her foot impatiently, waited for the elevator to come back down to her.

When the door opened she was disappointed to find it empty. "Damn," she said to herself. "He got off upstairs."

Mary then stepped into the elevator to go fetch her dog, aggravated by the chore.

The elevator ascended and she stepped out onto the second floor. Blackie was no where to be seen. As she started walking down the hall she spotted all the blood and stains where the men had killed different zombies a day earlier. As she turned down a split in the hall she spotted an empty wheelchair in an office. She looked down and her eyes took in the blood stains on the floor. This was where Scott died, she thought, as a tear rolled down her cheek. She wiped it away and continued looking for Blackie. A few minutes later she heard his barking. Moving quickly she followed the sound until she found him in an office at the end of the hall. He was just sitting there in front of a bathroom door growling. Mary jumped as the door shook on its hinges realizing what was in there.

"Come on boy, we need to go now." She said while tugging on the dog to leave with her. But Blackie would have none of it, he kept his butt planted firmly on the floor and continued to growl. His ears lowering until they were flat against his head. The zombie inside the bathroom heard the voices outside and renewed its attempts to break down the door. It hadn't had anything to eat since it had revived and the hunger inside it was unbearable.

With renewed strength it banged on the door harder.

Mary was about ready to give up and go retrieve one of the men to help her with Blackie when the hinges on the bathroom door finally gave out and the door fell out of the door frame.

The zombie rode the door as it fell out and landed on top of it as it hit the floor. Blackie didn't even hesitate; he jumped at the zombie and started chewing at its arms. For all the weight the animal had behind it the zombie shrugged it off and spotting Mary raised itself off the ground and started towards her.

Mary started backing up, unable to believe what was happening.

"Oh my God, not again." She said thinking back to the incident with the little girl. The zombie was getting closer by the second as Mary tried to back out of its reach. She looked at the nearest office desk for a weapon and spied a stapler. She reached down and grabbed it and threw it at the zombie with all her might. The stapler hit it in the forehead, leaving a gash on its skin but otherwise not doing any damage.

The zombie reached out to grab her as she dodged its hands. She grabbed a computer keyboard off the desk and yanked it free. As the zombie lunged for her she stepped back and then hit it in the face with the keyboard. The keyboard shattered against its head, the keys falling to the ground to be trampled moments later. Mary watched in horror as a G and an R stuck to the side of its face from the impact.

Blackie was down at the zombie's leg now, with his teeth firmly planted in its calf. Blackie was the only thing holding the zombie back from overwhelming Mary. Mary just kept grabbing things off of the desks and throwing it at the zombie; anything to slow it down.

Coffee mugs, ink blotters, pencils and pens. She even grabbed a stack of papers an inch high that was on one of the desks. Before she threw it her eyes caught the first words on it, "Dear Mr. Fulci," it said, before she threw it into the zombies face and distracted it for another precious few seconds.

Despite the weight of the dog the zombie was still making progress at reaching her. She didn't realize her feet had stepped on some of the keys from the broken keyboard until she felt her feet slip out from under her and she went crashing to the floor, hitting her head on the way down.

"Oh god," she thought, "I'm so dead."

She opened her eyes and watched as the zombie prepared to fall on her. But just before it did Blackie had backed up and had launched himself at the zombie, knocking it back to the floor with the weight of his body.

This time Blackie had the zombie by the neck and his jaws were clamped tight. Mary watched as the two struggled on the floor. When Mary saw the zombies claws starting to dig into Blackie's fur she knew she had to act. Picking herself up off the floor she spotted a letter opener on another desk. As fast as she could she ran over and grabbed it and then approached the zombie from the side and placed the letter opener by its ear, Then with all of her might she pressed it into its ear. A thin stream of blood poured out its ear as the letter opener slid all the way to its tip. Then just to make sure Mary twisted it, the blade shredding the zombie's brains inside its skull. The zombie immediately went slack, its hands falling to the floor.

Blackie seemed to sense that the fight was over and released his grip on its neck and sat back down onto the floor.

Mary too fell to the floor exhausted as the adrenaline drained out of her system now that she was safe.

The two of them sat there for awhile. Mary couldn't believe she was still alive. "Thank you boy," she said while rubbing his ears. "I don't know what I would've done with out you."

Blackie tried to lick her but she pulled her face away, laughing. "No thank you, I'll pass," she said. "But thanks for the thought."

Mary climbed back to her feet and together they walked back down the hall. The bond between them growing closer by the second

CHAPTER 46

THE SUN'S RAYS were pouring in through the office windows, hitting Henry in the face as he slept.

For a second he didn't know where he was. Was he in his own bed? Then reality came flooding back as he came to his senses.

Zombies, the constant threat of death and this uncomfortable office couch he had slept in. His back hurt, the couch he had slept on old and worn.

It was a pullout and due to its age sagged in the middle where the springs had stretched out.

Still it was better than the driver's seat in his now lost minivan.

He got up and walked to the bathroom, as he approached the doors he had already decided to use the men's room—yesterday's misadventure still fresh in his mind.

It was dark inside so he reached in and turned on the light. Empty. Just the way it should have been. He entered a stall and sat down, wincing as the cold toilet seat made contact with his flesh.

It was quiet in here, he thought, he could probably take a nap in here, especially if the lights were out. Then he heard the door open. His heart jumped into his throat.

"Oh Jesus Christ not again," he whispered.

Footsteps started coming closer to him. Then when he thought his heart would surely explode in his chest a voice said,"Hey Henry, you in here?"

Relief flooded through him as he recognized the voice. It was Jimmy. He hadn't realized he had been holding his breath and he let it out.

"God Jimmy, you nearly gave me a heart attack." He said. His heart was slowing back down to normal and he could now catch his breath.

"Sorry man." Jimmy said, oblivious. "Listen there's a few things we need to talk about."

"Fine, Jimmy, but can't it wait until I'm off the can?"

"Oh yeah sure, sorry Henry; look I'm gonna go lay down for a few more minutes. Can we talk when I get up?"

"No problem, I'll be around, I'm not going anywhere."

"I know you're not and that's exactly the problem." With that Jimmy left the bathroom, leaving Henry alone to ponder the last sentence spoken.

Henry finished up in the bathroom and then swung by the cafeteria for some breakfast. There was a phone on the wall and just for kicks he went over and picked it up, hoping there would be a dial tone.

Just as he expected he heard nothing but dead silence.

He shrugged as he hung the phone back on the wall. What did he expect? For an operator to be waiting for his call?

"How may I direct your call sir?" She'd say. And Henry would answer.

"Hi my name is Henry Watson could I please have the number for GET ME THE FUCK OUT OF HERE!"

Henry then sat down and had a meager breakfast of saltines and spam salvaged from his house.

After breakfast he went to the break room where he found it in total disarray. Henry entered the room and picked up a chair that was blocking the door and then went and sat down on the couch that was in the middle of the room.

In front of the couch on a small table sat a twelve inch television. He turned it on and starting flicking through channels until he had found a news station. Then he put the remote down and watched.

Surely there would be stories about what was going on, about what the military was doing. What about help for the survivors?

CHAPTER 47

JIMMY'S PLAN WAS simple, they would take as much food and water as they could carry and then head overland through the woods, staying out of sight of any army patrols until they had made it outside the quarantined area. Then they would make there way to the town's border. But this time they would be approaching from the uninfected side and should be safe from getting shot at by patrols. "But how will we explain how we got there?" Mary asked. "Especially because we'd be on foot."

That's the easiest part," Jimmy smiled, "We just say we were going to visit someone in town and our car broke down on the road."

Henry sat there, considering Jimmy's idea. "You know that just might work." He said.

Jimmy smiled as he sat back in his chair, proud of himself.

"So, when would we leave?" Mary inquired, looking at Jimmy and then Henry. "I say we stay here for a day or two and rest up. We finally have a safe place to stay and I don't want to throw that away so quick. What do you say Jimmy?" Henry asked him.

"Yeah its fine with me, besides my feet still hurt from the walk here," Jimmy replied.

"How about you Mary?" Henry asked her looking into her eyes.

"It's fine with me, the longer the better. I can't say I'm looking forward to running around in the woods again." she answered.

"Or shitting in them," Jimmy said as he smiled at Mary.

Mary put on a pretension of being annoyed but as Jimmy kept smiling at her she soon gave in and smiled too.

"Ha Ha, very funny," she said.

With that the meeting was over. The three of them each went there separate ways, Mary headed out to the lobby to check on Blackie, Jimmy went to the break room and Henry went to the cafeteria to finish the inventory on the food and water.

Later that day Henry caught up to Jimmy in the lobby.

"Hey Jimmy, what do you say we take care of that pile of corpses out back." Jimmy hesitated for a moment as he had a flashback of earlier that morning with his run in with the giant zombie. Then he shook it off and looked at Henry. "Ah, sure why not, I'll get the hotdogs." He said acting more cocky than he felt. The two of them walked outside together. It was a beautiful summer's day with not a cloud in the sky, a day that would fill you with hope.

As the two men walked around back they walked by Scott's grave. For a moment they just stood there, looking down on the mound where there friend was. Henry was the first to break the silence. With a slap to Jimmy's back he nodded in the direction of the corpses and together they continued on.

When they reached the pile of bodies the stench was incredible, and sitting out in the hot sun did nothing to help the problem. Henry used a bottle of lighter fluid he had found to spray the corpses and as he finished Jimmy lit a branch with a rag on the end to use as a safe way to start the fire.

When Henry was done he stepped back and waved to Jimmy to throw the torch. Jimmy threw the torch at the pile. It landed on the torso of what was once a lab assistant. The fluid soaked clothes immediately caught the flame and in moments the fire was burning well.

The two men stood there staring, locked in the hypnotic dance of the flames.

Then Jimmy broke the silence: "Hey Henry, did you ever imagine a few days ago that you'd be standing here doing this right now?"

His eyes never breaking contact with the flames Henry smiled.

"Jimmy my boy that is the understatement of the year."

As the wind shifted the two men had to put their sleeves over their mouths to try and cut down on the smoke and smell. The fire was burning strong now as the smell of charred meat filled the surrounding area.

Jimmy looked over at Henry and slapped him on the back.

"Well my deed is done, I'm going back inside."

Henry just nodded. "Go ahead. I'll be right behind you in a minute." "Jimmy walked away from the flames leaving Henry alone. Henry stood perfectly still as he stared at the fire. He swore as he watched he could see images dancing in the flames. He could see Emily waving to him. The kids he had seen in the fountain a few days ago floated by, only now they were beautiful children again. Not flesh eating monsters that would rip your throat out at a moments notice. As he continued to watch the flames he wandered if this was how an arsonist feels after setting his first fire, lost in the ever dancing and swirling flames. Finally he came to his senses and snapped out of it, rubbing his eyes from the strain of the images; or maybe it was just the smoke. He turned and followed Jimmy's footsteps back to the building.

The flames continued to burn, turning the corpses to ash which then floated away on the wind, scattering their remains across the field where they would then fall back to the ground and help to nurture the plant life.

The cycle of life marching forever forward, with or without mankind.

The next two days were mundane after everything that had happened to them. Jimmy had found a deck of cards during the exploration of the other rooms and that had kept the three of them busy for many an hour. The television in the break room was also a comfort, although there was still nothing on any of the channels about what had happened to their town.

They had discussed that oddity at supper the previous night.

"It just doesn't make any sense." Henry said while scooping a spoonful of baked beans into his mouth. "How can the government get away with a total media blackout?"

"Whether they can or can't is irrelevant, it's happening. I've tried my cell phone every chance I get and there's still no service." She stated.

"The way I see it, that can only help us." Jimmy said leaning back in his chair and folding his arms, his face looking like he had the answers to the universe.

"How so?" Mary asked sarcastically. "Please enlighten us with your wisdom. "Its simple, if know one out there knows what's going on around here, then once we get away who's going to question who we are or where we're from?"

Henry stared at him for a moment not quite grasping what Jimmy had said.

"It's simple Henry; as long as no one suspects we're from this town we're safe."

Henry and Mary looked at each other, and then Henry shrugged.

"Hopefully he's right, but if he's not our escape from here is going to be cut short a little quicker than we had planned."

"What do we have to lose?" Mary asked Henry.

"What's to lose? That's easy. If we lose, we die."

The three of them stayed silent after that; finishing the rest of their meal quietly as they each pondered their own fate.

CHAPTER 48

THE NEXT MORNING began like the others. Henry and Jimmy had gotten together after breakfast to play some cards, while Mary was in the lobby playing with Blackie. She would throw the plate and Blackie would catch it and then return it to her.

Like the others she was relaxing a little bit, finally feeling relatively safe in their own little haven in the woods.

That's why she was so startled when the silence of the lobby was shattered by the sound of vehicles pulling up to the front of the building.

She quickly ran to the lobby doors. Making sure she was hidden from sight from the outside, she peeked through to see who was out there.

Two pickup trucks and a couple of motorcycles had stopped in front in the driveway. Men were climbing off the back of the truck and the truck's interior was disgorging men as well. There must have been a group of at least twenty men out there in total; and all of them were armed.

The faces she saw were of hard men, most were wearing what appeared to be prison uniforms.

She could also see they were filthy, with at least a weeks worth of stubble on their faces. She was pretty sure if the door wasn't between them and her she would probably be able to smell them too. She took all this in within seconds as she backed away from the doors and ran as fast as she could to find Henry and Jimmy. Calling there names as she ran.

Henry and Jimmy heard her yelling as she was approaching the break room. Simultaneous with her frantic entry they rose to their feet.

She was running so fast she ran straight into Henry's arms.

"Whoa, what's the matter Mary?" Henry asked, perplexed by her actions.

"We got trouble. Out front, follow me, now." She panted; then took off towards the lobby, checking over her shoulder to make sure the two men were following her. Henry and Jimmy followed at a run only slowing down when she signaled them to get to cover as they approached the lobby doors.

They both crawled into a good position next to Mary to see the activity outside. It wasn't good.

"Shit, those guys do not look friendly; some of them must be escaped convicts." Henry whispered.

"Sure, makes sense," Jimmy said from his side. "When the shit hit the fan some of those guys took advantage of the situation and broke out of jail, or maybe it was one of those buses they use for transporting prisoners. They've probably been living on whatever they can loot from houses and stores for the past few days."

"So what are we going to do?" Mary asked.

"Simple, we're going to grab as much food and water as we can carry and get the hell out of here. There's to damn many of them, we wouldn't stand a chance if it came down to a fight." Henry said as he started backing away from the doors. "Come on people, let's move, we've only got minutes before they break in here and with the amount of guns they have we'd be slaughtered."

The two men headed to the cafeteria to collect supplies while Henry sent Mary to collect their weapons and the gear they would need on their trek through the woods.

Moments later they were gathered in the hallway all ready to go.

They all stopped at the sound of breaking glass coming from the lobby.

"Shit, they're in, they're not wasting anytime." Henry said. "Jimmy is there any other way out of here than through the lobby?"

Jimmy thought about it for a second. "We should be able to get out through the loading dock."

"Great, let's get moving." Henry replied. "Lead the way Jimmy; this is your building, after all."

Jimmy led them to the back end of the building. The further they got away from the lobby the more the sounds of destruction faded from hearing.

The loading dock was a wide open room with a little booth in the middle. There were two steel rollup doors, one for each bay. The bays were empty.

"Too bad there wasn't a truck in here, we could have used it to get away in." Jimmy said over his shoulder as they entered the room.

Jimmy jogged over to the small pedestrian door to the right of the metal bay doors and peeked out the window to get a clear view of the back of the building. What he saw wasn't good.

He waved to Henry to join him at the door.

Henry looked at Mary with a 'stay put' glance. She nodded and bent down to ruffle Blackie's fur.

"Shit, they're back here too." Henry said through gritted teeth." We're fuckin' trapped."

"We could try and make a run for it," Jimmy suggested.

"Yeah we could, but we probably wouldn't make it more than twenty feet before they cut us down." Henry answered back.

"Maybe we should just hide somewhere in the building and wait for them to leave." Mary suggested from across the room.

Henry considered it, weighing his options. There were too many to fight and they would probably kill both Jimmy and him if they got a hold of them. A group of twenty men with no laws to hold them back would probably do a lot worse to Mary than kill her. There was no way Henry was going to let that happen. There really weren't a lot of options to choose from. Mary's idea seemed sound. "Mary's right. Jimmy is there a place we can hold up until these assholes get tired and leave?" Henry asked, with concern clearly written on his face.

"Well, what about the basement?" Jimmy suggested.

"Yeah, that should work, lead on, we'll follow."

The three people weeded there way down the halls. Every corner they turned was a chance that they would be discovered. The tension was so sharp between the three companions you could almost taste it. A vast sigh of relief went through them when Jimmy finally stopped at a hatch on the floor. The hatch had a two inch thick padlock on it.

"This is it," he said, pulling the hatch open without any luck. "Shit it's locked. At Henry's questioning stare he continued. "The management started locking it after there were some unauthorized people found down there. You know, people making out and smoking dope and shit." He looked down at his feet embarrassed, even though the others had no idea what he meant.

"Great, what the fuck are we going to do now?" Henry yelled back at Jimmy and then caught himself and stopped. "Sorry Jimmy, that was uncalled for. It's just that we've been through so God dam much already . . ."

Jimmy held up his hand for Henry to stop talking and said: "Its cool Henry, we're all a little stressed."

Before he could continue they heard sounds coming from behind them.

"Shit they're coming, this way; I know how we can get around them." Jimmy said and led them further down the hall.

After a few lefts and rights Jimmy had led them back to where they had started. Hearing more sounds of banging and gunfire they ducked into one of the offices and closed and locked the door.

"What are they shooting at?" Mary asked from the back of the room. Blackie was leaning against her legs; he was quiet but could sense the tension in the air. "Probably nothing, men like that don't need a reason." Henry saw the scared look in Mary's eyes and went over to stand next to her. He reached out and put one hand on top of each of her shoulders and looked into her eyes.

"I won't let them hurt you, you know that right?" he asked her, holding her eyes with his own.

One small teardrop rolled down her face and she nodded yes.

Before anything else could be said they heard voices and banging coming from the hallway outside.

"Shit they're gonna be on us in a second. What the fuck are we gonna do?" Jimmy whispered with the sound of desperation clearly in his voice.

Henry looked around the room, racking his brain for a way out, and then his eye saw something.

"Hold on, I think I found us a way out." Henry said with a smile; and then got busy formulating their escape.

CHAPTER 49

PRISONER #9002001, AKA JOHN "Sleepy" Higgins walked down the hallway of the building he and his buddies were presently ransacking. So far they hadn't found anything of value.

He was a big man at 6'2' and his shoulders were wide. His arms were like steel cables from all the weight lifting he had done back in the yard. He had been serving life without the possibility of parole. When the guards had all started dropping dead and then coming back to life it was quite easy to kill them again. Hell, he hadn't even realized some of the guards were zombies until one of his buddies had pointed it out to him. Shit, he had just thought he was killing people. He liked killing people. Now there was no law around but his own. He liked that. Unfortunately there still hadn't been anything to kill here, either human or zombie. Although he had hope that maybe behind the next door there'd be something to shoot.

His Momma had always said it was good to have hope.

He came up to the next door in the hallway—did he hear movement behind the door?—and got ready to kick it in. His buddies were doing the same thing to the other doors on this floor.

His foot slammed into the door right by the latch, the door flying in amidst splinters.

He looked into the room and came face to face with a big black Labrador retriever. The dog didn't even hesitate as its haunches tensed and the dog went flying at him. He already had his rifle up and as the dog was about to strike him he squeezed the trigger, the bullets hitting the dog in the middle of its chest.

The dog still barreled into him due to the momentum of its body, but was already dead as it struck him; though the impact still knocked him to the floor. He brushed it off as some of his buddies came over to see what had happened.

"Just a fucking dog," he said, "You assholes quit fucking around and keep looking for something good to kill. Oh Yeah, and find some fucking water too."

He walked back into the office the dog had come from to investigate further but it was empty.

He turned around and left, moving on to the next room, his bloodlust far from satiated.

The room the big man had just vacated was quiet. Empty. Nothing was in it to call attention to itself.

Perhaps if he had stood in the center of the room and looked up at the ceiling he might have noticed a ventilation duct cover slightly askew. And if he had looked real close he might have seen a face hiding behind that duct cover; a face with tears running down its cheeks.

Just before the office door was kicked in Henry had noticed the ventilation duct on the ceiling.

Immediately he had pushed the desk under it and with a chair perched on the desk he had been able to pry it off and get the group inside.

"Wait, what about Blackie?" Mary asked, her eyes pleading.

"I'm sorry Mary there's no time," he said as he pushed her butt into the duct. Jimmy had been the first one in and had grabbed Mary's hand to pull her up. The duct divided about six feet down and Jimmy was able to let Mary get by him so he could crawl back up to grab Henry's hand.

Henry stood on the chair and as Jimmy pulled him up he used his feet to kick the chair off the desk to disguise where they were. Henry looked down over his shoulder; Blackie was sitting there watching him as he was being pulled into the duct, his tale happily wagging behind him.

Henry's eyes met Blackies' and his heart broke. "I'm so sorry boy," he said. Then he was inside the duct and climbing over Jimmy so he could turn around and face forward. He wanted to see what was happening. Jimmy had just gotten the duct cover secured when they heard someone right outside the door. As Jimmy and Henry changed places in the duct the door suddenly flew in and Blackie jumped up at the man in the door and attacked him only to be shot down. Henry felt the loss of the animal deep into his soul, although the dog had only been with them for a few days he had already grown attached to him, not to mention how attached Mary had gotten to him. Leaving him behind was like leaving one of their own to die in the office.

But he had know choice, there was no way they could have possibly gotten Blackie into the duct in time and even had they managed it, there's no way the dog would have been silent.

Still, rationalizing it didn't make him feel any better.

Now all they could do was sit and wait and hope the men outside in the hallways would get bored with this place and move on to find better spoils elsewhere. Henry got comfortable in the duct, trying not to move much and give there position away. He could hear Jimmy's breathing behind him in the confines of the small ventilation shaft.

No one talked as the echo could give away their hiding place. Crashing sounds mixed with yelling voices continued and then gradually faded away. The hours passed by, and with nothing to do but lay there the adrenaline soon left their systems, leaving them exhausted.

The air in the duct was stuffy and soon the combination of exhaustion and inactiveness had made everyone drowsy and in no time they had all drifted off into a restless sleep.

When Henry came awake he had no idea what time it was, as he peeked out of the duct cover he could see the sun was still up, though its rays seemed fainter, as if it was late in the afternoon.

He could hear the others stirring behind him and waited for them to come awake as well.

"What time is it?" Mary asked her voice a whisper in the confines of the duct.

"I'm not sure, after noontime definitely but I don't know by how much. I left my watch in the break room when we had to take off." Henry whispered back.

"I have to go to the bathroom." Jimmy said from behind him.

"How's Blackie Henry? Is he ok? I haven't heard him since we got up here." Mary asked.

Henry thought about the answer he was going to give her. He didn't need her freaking out in the duct and giving them away, but he also didn't want to lie to her. So he opted with denial.

"I don't know Mary, I haven't seen him, he probably got away. I'm sure he's fine. "Jimmy cleared his voice. "Excuse me people; I said I have to go to the bathroom."

"So what to you want me to do about it," Henry snapped back. "Hold it in, good God Jimmy if they find us they're gonna kill us."

"No you don't understand Henry, I really have to piss, and I had to go before we climbed up in here but there wasn't time to go. It went away for awhile but now its back and I really have to go now." The last six words were spoken slowly so he could emphasize the importance of them.

"I haven't heard anything in a while Henry, maybe they're gone." Mary whispered. "Yeah and maybe there not which means if they're still here we'll be seen and all this shit will have been for nothing."

"Well make up your mind quick old man because I'm ready to blow." Jimmy said. The truth was he hadn't heard anything either. Only a short time had passed since he had woken up and he should have heard something, anything, if they were still in the building.

But to tell the truth he didn't want to go out there, it was safe in this duct and that part of the survival instinct inside him that dictates fight or flight had found one more option. Sit and wait.

After another minute Jimmy prodded his butt with his hand to force a decision out of him.

"Fine, all right, I'll check and see if it's clear. But you two stay put until I get back. If you hear anything stay quiet, At least they won't get you too."

"Yeah, yeah, just hurry up. And come right back if it's clear. I'm ready to piss my pants."

"You'd better not Jimmy, I'll kill you if you do." Mary said from behind him.

Her face was directly behind him with the way their bodies were positioned in the duct

Henry pried the duct cover off and stuck his head out into the room.

Nothing, there was no sound that he could discern but the buzzing of the flies that had found Blackie's body.

Slowly he climbed out of the duct and when he was hanging above the desk he let go. Landing on the desk he immediately jumped down onto the floor and crouched behind it. He then waited to see if extricating himself from the duct had called any attention to himself. After a few agonizing seconds had passed by uneventfully he raised him self up and proceeded to the door.

The door was hanging by one hinge as he walked by it and out into the hallway. He cocked his ear in the direction of the lobby but no sound came to him. He quickly but quietly headed down to the lobby. The hallway was in total disarray, with books and paper scattered everywhere. As he walked by the other offices and rooms he saw similar signs of destruction. It was like a tornado had blown through. He approached the metal double doors that separated his hallway with the lobby and peeked around them. The lobby was deserted.

With his heart in his throat he ran across the lobby to the now shattered glass doors and looked out. The driveway was empty, nothing to show there had been vehicles there except the churned up sod on the sides where a careless driver had driven over it.

Relief flooded through him as he quickly ran back to the others to tell them it was safe.

"Its ok, it looks like there gone." Henry called out to the open duct.

Before the last word he had spoken had finished leaving his lips Jimmy's face came out of the duct. Then the way only youth will allow he grabbed the end of the duct and flipped himself out. As he landed on the desk he was still in motion as he ran for the bathroom, almost knocking Henry over in his mad dash. Then Mary's face poked out; before Henry could say anything to her she had spotted Blackie in the hallway.

Her hand went to her face as shock and sadness overwhelmed her and she started crying.

Henry climbed up on the desk and helped her down. Once she was out she buried her face in his chest and continued to cry. They stood there for a few moments until Jimmy walked in, he had also seen Blackie on the floor and his face showed the sorrow he felt.

The three of them stood there for a few seconds more and then Henry disengaged Mary from him and looked at Jimmy. "Give me a hand with him?" Henry said, motioning to Blackie.

"Of course, I'll get a blanket or something so we can move him."

Jimmy went off to retrieve one.

Henry turned to look at Mary and said: "Mary he was a good dog, a brave dog, I'll miss him too, I'm so sorry."

She just nodded, accepting his condolences, then with tears still rolling down her eyes she walked out of the room and walked out into the lobby. Jimmy returned with an old tarp and the two of them got to work wrapping Blackie up in it.

Henry sighed to himself; time to bury another friend.

As he rolled the body into the tarp he could feel the tears welling up inside him. Not just for Blackie, but for everyone else he'd lost. And all the innocent people who had died horribly in the past few days, and quite possibly for the world itself. The two of them lifted the carcass up and together they carried it outside to place in the ground next to Scott.

CHAPTER 50

AFTER BLACKIE WAS buried the three companions went back inside the building to decide their fate.

As they stood around the lobby desk Jimmy was the first one to speak.

"I say its time we get out of here, the doors are broken and the place is a shit hole now. We don't have a lot of water left thanks to those assholes taking it all. So what's the point in staying?"

"I agree" said Mary, "this place was almost our tomb. It's too big to defend, and Henry, Jimmy is right about the water situation. "I know, I know," Henry sighed, "It's just that we had finally found a place that was at least a little safe from all the shit going on out there." Henry waved his arm out at the woods and beyond. "It was nice to take a breather. "Yeah well breather's over, old man, 'cause we're not safe here anymore, what happens if the army comes next time or some other nutcases. No, we need to get out of the infected zone and fast or we're all gonna die here."

"All right, let's gather as much stuff as we can and then head out. If we leave within the hour we should have a few hours of day light left until night falls. "The three of them headed off in different directions to retrieve their weapons and see what might be left after the place had been ransacked.

Mary kicked something on her way out of the lobby and stopped cold when she saw what it was.

The plastic plate she and Blackie had played with.

She felt herself tearing up again and fought it back down. She had cried enough for a while.

She threw the plate one more time imagining Blackie running to catch it. But he wasn't there and the plate bounced off the wall and lay still; which was where she left it.

Henry was just about finished, he had retrieved their weapons from the office they had hid in and then went down to the cafeteria to see if anything could be salvaged.

There was nothing left, the place was totally cleared out, not to mention totally destroyed. The table was smashed to rubble as was the steam table. The refrigerator had been toppled over, the contents that weren't desired tossed on the ground, where they would soon start to rot.

Yeah, Henry thought, it was definitely time to move on.

He shouldered the backpacks and headed off to the lobby to rendezvous with his friends.

Jimmy had headed for the break room after he had vacated the lobby, as he walked down the hallway he had to constantly walk around or kick something out of his way that was blocking his path.

"Shit, these guys did a number on this place." He muttered to himself as he pushed an office chair out of his way.

When he arrived at the break room he first had to pry open the door as it was jammed. When he pushed as hard as he could and was able to squeeze through the opening he quickly found out what the problem was.

There was a dead body in front of the door; its weight had been holding the door closed.

Jimmy stepped over the corpse and then took a closer look. The poor bastard had half his face blown off. Maybe an altercation gone wrong, Jimmy thought if this was what they did to friends then Jimmy was glad they hadn't found him and his companions when they were hiding.

As he looked around the room he didn't see much of interest to take with him. He found a cigarette lighter on the floor and a roll of paper towels in the corner under an end table.

He grabbed it and tossed it in the air and caught it, "Cool" he said, "Better than leaves to wipe my ass with in the woods."

As he turned over a chair he spotted the remote for the television. He picked it up off the floor and after looking at it for a moment he tossed it onto the corpse, then he set the television on the floor in front of the body and turned it on. The TV buzzed for a second and then flicked on. The picture was terrible due to the beating it had recently taken but it was still viewable.

"Here you go pal something to keep you company." Jimmy said as he walked out of the room to rendezvous with the others.

As Jimmy slipped back through the door he pulled it closed after him. The corpse slumped back to the ground. On the television a blurry weatherman was droning on about storm clouds and high pressure areas until the back of the television started shooting sparks out the back.

And then the picture went dark.

When they were once again gathered in the lobby together and each had filled the others in on their findings they took one last look around the lobby and then walked out of the shattered doors.

As the group walked single file through the doors with the glass crunching under their feet they went around the side of the building to pay their respects to their lost comrades one final time.

They gathered around the two graves and stood silent for a moment, then as one they walked off into the woods. They had lost two good friends within forty-eight hours and were now heading back into unknown territory. They could only hope that was the last of the casualties their group would suffer in this war for survival they had now found themselves in.

The woods beckoned to them of a destiny unsure in its outcome. The clear blue sky filled them with hope. They didn't know what the future held for them, but they did know that whatever happens they would face it head on and as a team. And god help any who got in their way.

CHAPTER 51

EPILOGUE

THE TOWN'S WATER supply was surrounded on all sides by barbed wire. Men in white hazmat suits and oxygen masks scurried around taking samples and comparing notes. The lake was now a dark green color as the mutated bacteria had now fully contaminated it.

Soldiers also dressed in white suits and masks also patrolled the perimeter, keeping any unwanted visitors away; either living or dead.

Every once in a while a shot would ring out as a soldier shot a wandering zombie.

Professor Sebastian Keagan always wondered if the shot had killed a live person or a walking dead one, unfortunately at the moment both being the same thing in the military's eyes

He had been called into this quiet little town almost three days ago.

Working with the findings that Dr. Martin had sent him before he went missing Professor Keagan had been able to isolate the mutated bacteria and he now believed he had come up with a solution. It would only take a matter of days to correct this little environmental mistake and then he would be able to return to his state of the art lab in San Francisco and continue his own work.

Colonel Miller would be pleased with his results.

Everything would be fine, the government would make up some story about chlorine gas or a radiation leak to placate the public and within a few weeks the story would wind up on the back pages of newspapers all over America.

He smiled to himself. The American public got bored so quickly.

On completion of this project he was promised a large bonus. In his mind he was already spending it on much needed tools for his lab back home.

He reconsidered maybe taking a little vacation after he left here. Why not? There wasn't that much of a hurry to get back. His assistants could keep his research moving forward for another week or so.

His mother used to have a saying,"What's the rush? You've got all the time in the world."

At this precise moment in time he felt exactly that way.

Professor Keagan strolled out of the tent he had been working in for most of the day. It felt good to be outside, even if he couldn't feel the air on his face through the mask.

That was all right, he could still see the sky. He barely looked up long enough to notice the clouds were becoming thicker over the lake area.

He didn't notice the small flashes of lightning, or hear the soft sounds of thunder as the sound rolled across the sky.

He then turned back around and reentered the tent to return to work.

If Professor Keagan had paid more attention to the clouds he would have noticed that they had taken on a green tint as the bacteria within the lake slowly suffused the clouds with the evaporating lake water; and as the wind blew, the clouds started drifting away from the lake area and out across the countryside where they would then mingle with other air currents and then continue on their journey, going from state to state until the whole of the Midwest would be affected.

If Professor Keagan had paid more attention to the sky instead of focusing his attention on the ground he may have noticed one more very important thing.

It looked like rain.

THE END?

Bad Moon Rising

Frances di Plino

"I loved this tense, fast-paced
and gripping novel.
A brilliant debut."
Amanda Hodgkinson
New York Times Bestselling author of
22 Britannia Road

"sensational, a complete hit...truly thrilling"
Bethan Townsend
Judging Covers Reviews

"With memorable characters and a plot that keeps the reader guessing right to the very end, Frances di Plino's debut novel, Bad Moon Rising, will more than satisfy any fan of good crime writing."
Jo Reed
Author of the Blood Dancer series of novels

Copyright © 2012 by Frances di Plino
Cover design by Jane Dixon-Smith and Billy Alexander
Cover art by Crooked Cat
All rights reserved.

ISBN: 978-1-908910-40-0
No part of this book may be used or reproduced in any manner whatsoever without written permission of the author or Crooked Cat Publishing except for brief quotations used for promotion or in reviews. This is a work of fiction. Names, characters, places, and incidents are used fictitiously. Any resemblance to actual persons living or dead, business establishments, events, or locales, is entirely coincidental.

First Black Line Edition, Crooked Cat Publishing Ltd. 2013

Discover us online
www.crookedcatpublishing.com

Join us on facebook:
www.facebook.com/crookedcatpublishing

Tweet a photo of yourself holding this book to **@crookedcatbooks** and something nice will happen.